U0165801

TOEICmate Series

NEW TOEIC
新多益測驗解析

高志豪 著

五南圖書出版公司 印行

Acknowledgments

The following individuals provided invaluable assistance in the development of this book:
Thomas J. Brink, Terri Pebsworth, David McCornick, Jane Munro,

ETS, the ETS logo, and TOEIC are registered trademarks of Educational Testing Service.
This publication is not endorsed or approved by ETS.

All right reserved. No part of this work may be reproduced, transcribed, or used in any form or by any means—graphic, electronic , or mechanical, including photocopying, recording, taping, Web distribution, or information storage and retrieval systems—without the prior written permission of the publisher.

copyright © 2008 *GLOBALmate* Co., LTD.
ISBN: 978-986-83023-9-6

Websites below for reference:

 http://www.toeic.com.tw

 http://www.toeicok.com.tw

 http://www.englishok.com.tw

 http://www.toeicmate.com.tw

http://vip.englishok.com.tw

序

　　本書包含了三部份，一為多益測驗的題型介紹，一為多益測驗常出現的片語、單字等。另外加上一組完整的仿真測驗題（200 題），以供讀者們實作模擬測驗，並附上翻譯、解答和字表，裨使讀者們查考。

　　但是，筆者必須誠實地提醒讀者們，只讀一本書、只作一組試題，而妄想得高分，是不可能的。最好在英語學習方面下一番工夫，尋求適合自己的學習方法和模式，縮短學習的進程、多作練習，讓學習更有效率！

高志豪

2016 年 2 月 16 日

CONTENTS

題解篇

New TOEIC 聽力測驗常出現的
Idioms 習慣語

A

---

001. **a bit**　有點兒，稍微

例 I'm feeling a bit tired.

註 tired *a.* 疲勞的；令人厭煩的 ／ be tired of 對⋯感到厭煩

---

002. **afford to**　買（付）得起

例 Their company simply can not afford to pay overtime.

註 simply *adv.* 僅僅；完全地，的確 ／ overtime *n.* 加班；加班費

---

003. **all at once**　同時

例 All at once many things happened and I was confused by them.

註 confused *a.* 迷惑不解的；混亂的 ／ once and for all 永遠地，徹底地

---

004. **apply for**　申請⋯

例 What position did he apply for?

註 position *n.* 職位；位置 ／ apply to 向⋯申請；適用；適宜

---

005. **as of / as from**　自⋯起

例 This shopping mall will be open as of June.

註 mall *n.* 購物商場，購物中心 ／ opening *n.* 開幕(啟用)典禮

---

006. assemble ~ for   為⋯召集

例 We'll assemble a task force for this portfolio project.

註 task force 專案小組，特別小組 ／ portfolio **n.** 投資組合

007. assign to   指派⋯

例 Two senior consultants were assigned to the firm's branch in Hong Kong.

註 senior **a.** 高級的；年長的；資深的 ／ consultant **n.** 顧問

008. at a time   每次，一次

例 Applicants will be interviewed separately, one at a time.

註 applicant **n.** 申請人 ／ separately **adv.** 分開地；獨立地

009. at the latest   最晚，最遲

例 Audrey promised she'd arrive by 9 o'clock at the latest.

註 promise **v.** 承諾，答應 ／ compromise **n.** 妥協，折衷

010. away from   離⋯

例 She turned away from the door and went over to the back of the house.

註 go over 走到 ／ back **n.** (建築物)後面

011. be about to   正要⋯

例 They arrived just as the wedding reception was about to begin.

註 reception **n.** 招待會，歡迎會；宴會 ／reception room 會客室，客廳

012. **be allergic to**　對…極反感

例 He is allergic to passive smoking.

註 allergic *a.* 極反感的；過敏的 ／ passive smoking 二手煙

013. **be away on business**　出差

例 Martin will be away on business for several days.

註 on business 出差 ／ be in business 已經營業

014. **be bound for**　前往…的

例 The container ship was bound for Mexico.

註 container *n.* 貨櫃 ／ I'm bound to say ~ 我得說…

015. **be concerned about**　擔心…

例 I'm concerned about her safety in this stormy night.

註 concerned *a.* 擔心的 ／ stormy *a.* 暴風雨的

016. **be crowded with**　擠滿

例 The department store was crowded with hundreds of people.

註 department store 百貨公司 ／ crowded *a.* 滿滿的；擁擠的

017. **be due**　預定

例 A copy of the latest edition of our magazine will be due next week.

註 latest *a.* 最新的，最近的 ／ edition *n.* 一期(版) ／ due *a.* 預定的

018. **be eager to** 熱切⋯，渴望⋯

例 Our sales force is eager to expand into new markets.

註 sales force 銷售團隊 ／ expand *v.* 拓展，擴張

019. **be good at** 精通⋯，熟練⋯

B

例 She is good at languages.

註 language *n.* 語言 ／ be good about 樂於⋯

020. **be pleased to** 高興⋯

例 I'm pleased to announce the champion of the marathon.

註 announce *v.* 宣佈，宣告 ／ champion *n.* 冠軍 ／ marathon *n.* 馬拉松

021. **be qualified to** 勝任⋯的，有資格⋯

例 I'm well qualified to give an opinion.

註 qualified *a.* 合格的，有資格的 ／ opinion *n.* 看法；主張；見解

022. **be suitable for** 適合⋯，適宜⋯

例 Adult magazines are not suitable for children.

註 suitable *a.* 適合的，適宜的 ／ suited *a.* 合適的，適當的

023. **be supposed to** 應該⋯

例 We are supposed to go to Jane's farewell party on Saturday night.

註 farewell *a.* 告別的 ／ farewell speech 告別演說

024. be sure to 一定要…

例 Be sure to finish off the project by Friday.

註 finish off 完成 ／ finish up 最後到達(處於)，完成，結束

025. be worth ~ing 值得…

例 This novel is definitely worth reading.

註 definitely *adv.* 毫無疑問；確定地 ／ worthless *a.* 無價值的，無用的

026. behind schedule / time 比預定時間晚

例 The express train arrived behind schedule.

註 express *a.* 快速的 ／ schedule *n.* 日程表；*v.* 排定 ／ scheduled *a.* 定期的，預定的

027. by the way 順便一提

例 By the way, Smith wants you to call him back.

註 call sb. back 回…電話 ／ call for 要求 ／ call off 取消

028. cater to 迎合…，投合…

例 She refused to cater to customers' ridiculous demands.

註 cater *v.* 滿足…的需要 ／ ridiculous *a.* 荒唐的；可笑的；荒謬的

029. check in 辦理登機手續

例 We should check in at the airport at least 3 hours before our flight.

註 flight *n.* 飛行，飛航；航班 ／ check out 結帳離開 ↔ check in 登記住宿

030. **close down** 倒閉，關閉

例 | Their company has decided to close down its New York branch.

註 | branch *n.* 分公司，分支機構 ／ close up 關門，打烊

031. **come along** 進行，進展

例 | How's Bill coming along with his skating?

註 | skate *v.* 溜冰 ／ come about (偶然)發生 ／ come across 偶然遇見

032. **come by** 拜訪…

例 | I'll come by your office this morning, and we can talk over coffee.

註 | talk over ~ 邊…邊談 ／ come about 比…更重要

033. **come into effect** 開始實施（生效）

例 | The tax increase came into effect on New Year's Day.

註 | increase *n.* 增加 ／ effect *n.* 效果 ／ in effect 實際上，事實上

034. **come up with** 想出，提出

例 | Is that the novel solution he came up with?

註 | novel *a.* 新的，新奇的 ／ solution *n.* 解決方法 ／ come under 遭到

035. **deal with** 處理，應對

例 | The mayor spent the day with his consultants discussing how to deal with the problem of traffic jams.

註 | mayor *n.* 市長 ／ traffic jam 交通堵塞(擁擠) ／ deal in 經營，交易；讓…參加

036. **due to** 因為，由於

例 The company's bad finances were due to poor management.

註 finances *n.* 財務狀況，經濟狀況 ／ due *a.* 到期的；應完成的

037. **end up ~ing** 最後⋯

例 We ended up spending the day at the beach.

註 beach *n.* 海灘 ／ end in 以⋯結束 ／ in the end 最後，終於

038. **every other day** 每隔一天

例 The doctor told her to take the medicine every other day.

註 take the medicine 服藥，吃藥 ／ every last 每個(用於強調)

039. **fall behind** 落後

例 Julian was tired and started to fall behind the rest of the runners.

註 rest *n.* 剩餘，其餘(部份) ／ at rest 停止的，靜止的

040. **fall through** 失敗，終成泡影

例 The deal fell through and his company went bankrupt.

註 bankrupt *a.* 破產的 ／ fall off 降低，下降，減少

041. **far away** 遠處

例 From far away the fire engines' sirens were wailing.

註 siren *n.* (警車、消防車等的)警報器 ／ wail *v.* 呼嘯，慟哭

D
E
F

042. **feel free to**　隨意，不受限

例 Feel free to come and go as you please!

註 free **a.** 自由的；不受限制的；隨意的 ／ free gift 贈品

043. **figure out**　理解…，明白…

例 I couldn't figure out what he was talking about.

註 figure **v.** 認為；估計；揣測 ／ It figures that~ 有道理，果不其然

044. **fill in for**　暫代…

例 She will fill in for the receptionist next week.

F

註 receptionist **n.** 接待員，櫃檯人員 ／ fill up 加滿，裝滿

045. **fill out**　填寫…

例 It took me an hour to fill out the order form.

註 order **n.** 訂單，訂貨 ／ fill in the blanks 填補空白，補充說明

046. **find out**　查明…，發現…

例 The police may never find out the truth about the murder.

註 murder **n.** 謀殺(案) ／ find one's way 設法到達

047. **for a while**　一段時間

例 The auto company was offering test drive programs for a while.

註 auto **n.** 汽車 ／ offer **v.** 提供；給予 ／ test drive 試車，試開

048. **for ages** 很長一段時間

例 She's worked here for ages.

註 ages **n.** 很長的一段時間 ／ in ages 很久以來

049. **for sale** 待售，出售中

例 Those samples of curtain fabrics are not for sale.

註 curtain **n.** 窗簾 / fabric **n.** 布料；織物 / on sale (美) = on offer (英) 降價出售

050. **get into** 投入（事情等）

例 His young brother is really getting into the Internet.

註 Internet **n.** 網路，網際網路 / get on with 進行，開展(某事)

F
G

051. **get rid of** 擺脫…，丟棄…

例 She just sat there chattering all day and we couldn't get rid of her.

註 chatter **v.** 嘮叨，喋喋不休 / be rid of 擺脫

052. **get through** 熬過（困境）

例 He will need his friends' support to get through his depression.

註 support **n.** 支持 / depression **n.** 沮喪，消沉；蕭條，不景氣

053. **go out of business** 停業，倒閉

例 The supermarket has gone out of business.

註 supermarket **n.** 超市，超商 / business day = working day 上班日

054. go over 仔細檢查…

例 They went over everything about my project, down to the last detail.

註 down to the last detail 下至(包括)細微末節 / go into detail (about / on) 詳細敘述

055. hold on to = hold onto 保留（住）…

例 He managed to hold on to his job when Norma lost hers.

註 manage to 勉強做到；做成，辦到 / all is not lost 還有一絲成功的希望

056. in (with) reference to 關於…

例 In reference to new market analysis, we want to discuss with you.

註 reference *n.* 提及，提到 / analysis *n.* 分析 / analyst *n.* 分析家，分析員

G
H
I

057. in a good mood 好心情（情緒）

例 I had never seen her in such a good mood before.

註 mood *n.* 心情，情緒 / creat (set) a mood 營造氛圍

058. in addition 另外，此外

例 You can gain valuable work experience and, in addition, you can get some good contacts.

註 contact *n.* (有用的)社會關係 / contact lens 隱形眼鏡

059. in advance 事先，預先

例 The first phase's details of the project had been circulated well in advance.

註 phase *n.* 階段；時期 / circulate *v.* 散發，散佈；流傳

060. in charge of 負責…，管理…

例 Miss Daiwin is in charge of the sales department.

註 charge *n.* 管理；感染力 ／ sales clerk (美) = sales assistant 售貨員，店員

061. in good shape （健康）狀況良好

例 Due to eating a balanced diet, she is in good shape now.

註 balanced *a.* 均衡的 ／ diet *n.* 飲食，食物 ／ shape *n.* 狀況，情況

062. in person 親自

例 I'm kind of busy today and I can't attend the meeting in person.

註 kind of = somewhat 有點兒 ／ attend *v.* 參加 ／ attendant *n.* 服務員

063. keep sth in mind 記得（住）…

例 Keep it in mind that you have to attend the meeting on Friday.

註 mind *n.* 心思；注意力 ／ to my mind 我認為，依我看來

I
K

064. keep track of 掌握…訊息（線索）

例 To keep track of all our expenses is important.

註 track *n.* 痕跡；訊息 ／ expenses *n.* 支出，花費

065. keep up with 趕上…，跟上…

例 John had to hurry to keep up with them.

註 hurry *v.* 急忙，匆忙 ／ hurry up = make haste = hasten 趕緊，趕快

066. leaf through 匆匆翻閱…

例 She leafed through the fashion magazine and didn't buy it.

註 fashion **n.** 時尚；時裝 ／ after the fashion of ~ 模仿…的風格

067. let go 解雇

例 Smith was let go after he was charged with the theft of club funds.

註 charge **v.** 指控 ／ theft **n.** 竊盜(行為) ／ funds **n.** 資金，現金

068. look for 尋找…

例 I spent lots of time looking for clues as to his identity.

註 clue **n.** 線索 ／ identity n. 身份 ／ corporate identity 企業形象識別

069. look forward to 期待…，盼望…

例 Carol was looking forward to her retirement.

註 retirement **n.** 退休(生活) ／ come out of retirement 復出

070. look over 瀏覽…

例 I've looked over his pet project he'd completed earlier.

註 pet project 最喜愛的事 ／ pet theory (subject) 一貫的主張

L
M

071. make out 理解…，看（聽）出…

例 I can just make out a few words on this page.

註 a few 幾個；一些 ／ make up for 彌補，補償

072. **make sure** 查明…，弄清楚…

例 We'd better make sure we locked the door.

註 lock *v.* 鎖 ／ lock in profits (gains) 長期獲利

073. **make up** 捏造…，編造…

例 She made up some excuse about her watch not working.

註 excuse *n.* 藉口，理由 ／ watch *n.* 手錶

074. **manage to** 總算…

例 Amanda had somehow managed to finish her assignment.

註 somehow *adv.* 以某種方法 ／ assignment *n.* 作業；分派的任務(工作)

075. **not ~ at all** 一點也不…

例 She doesn't know anything at all about computers.

註 computer dating 電腦擇友 ／ computerize *v.* 使電腦化

076. **on behalf of** 代表…

例 On behalf of everyone here, I'd like to welcome our special guest, Doctor Clifford Kurtt.

註 behalf *n.* 代替(表)…；為了幫助… ／ guest worker 外籍勞工

M
N
O

077. **on duty** 值勤（班）

例 He fell asleep while on duty.

註 duty *n.* 責任，義務 ／ duties *n.* 職責 ／ off duty 下班，不值班

078. **on foot**　步行

例 In a traffic jam, it's easier to get here on foot than by car.

註 traffic jam 交通堵塞(擁擠) ／ put one's foot in one's mouth 說錯話

079. **on one's own**　獨自

例 Carol did it all on her own.

註 all on one's own = all alone = completely alone 獨自

080. **on sale**　出售

例 Our new coffee machines are on sale all throughout this month.

註 throughout *prep.* 在整個期間；*adv.* 整個，自始至終

081. **on schedule / time**　準時

例 The project was completed on schedule.

註 schedule *n.* 日程表，時間表 ／ complete and utter 徹頭徹尾的

082. **on target**　實現目標

例 The season's sales figure was on target.

註 figure *n.* 數字 ／ target date 預定日期

083. **on the way (to)**　在路上

例 On the way home I met an old friend.

註 ways and means 方法，辦法，途徑

084. **out of business**　停業，倒閉

例 A lot of small companies went out of business during the economic depression.

註 depression *n.* 蕭條，不景氣 ／ economic *a.* 經濟的 ／ economical *a.* 節儉的

085. **out of control**　失去控制

例 The economist predicts that the inflation will get out of control.

註 economist *n.* 經濟學家 ／ predict *v.* 預言，預知 ／ inflation *n.* 通貨膨脹

086. **out of order**　壞了

例 The elevator was out of order and they had to walk to the sixth floor.

註 elevator *n.* (美)電梯 ／ lift *n.* (英)電梯

087. **pay for**　支付…

例 Let me pay for lunch.

註 pay with 用…支付 ／ pay the bill 付帳 ／ pay for itself 自己賺回成本

088. **pay off**　清償…，還清…

例 How soon does she have to pay off the loan?

註 loan *n.* 貸款，借款 ／ pay out 花費，支付(巨款)；回收

089. **pick up**　開車接人

例 Will you pick up my son after lunch?

註 pick out 挑出，挑選 ／ pick over 精挑細選 ／ pick through 搜尋

O
P

090. **plan to** 打算…

例 Our president is planning to retire at 60.

註 retire *v.* 退休 ／ retiree *n.* 退休者 ／ retirement home 養老院

P
R
S

091. **plug into** 與…相連接，參與…

例 With novel products, his company is obviously hoping to plug into the international market.

註 novel = new *a.* 新的，新奇的 ／ novelty *n.* 新奇的事物 ／ obviously *adv.* 明顯地

092. **pull over** 靠邊停車

例 The police signaled frantically to her to pull over.

註 signal *v.* 打信號(手勢)，示意 ／ frantically *adv.* 緊急匆忙地，忙亂地

093. **put off** 延後(期)…

例 He'll have to put off his visit until next week.

註 on a visit 拜訪 ／ put at 計算 ／ put in (into) 投入(時間、精力)

094. **rather than** 而非…

例 They want serious financial troubles settled sooner rather than later.

註 trouble 問題，困難 ／ be in trouble 遇上麻煩(困境) ／ settle *v.* 解決

095. **settle on** 決定…，選定…

例 His new book has yet to settle on a title.

註 settle in (into) (使)適應… ／ settle up with 和…結帳

096. slip one's mind / memory　被忘記，被忽略

例　Her birthday completely slipped my mind.

註　slip in 插入(話語) ／ slip into 逐漸陷入(不好狀況)

097. take / make a stand　採取（表明）立場

例　She'll have to take a stand on the question of the union election.

註　take a stand on 表明對⋯的立場 ／ take a stand against 表明⋯反對的立場

S
T

098. take ~ apart　拆開⋯

例　In order to fix her computer, he had to take it apart.

註　fix **v.** 修理 ／ take down 拆除，拆卸 ／ take on (開始)僱用；呈現

099. take care of　照顧⋯，照料⋯，負責處理⋯

例　We'll leave Peter to take care of the refreshments.

註　refreshments **n.** 點心，茶點 ／ refresh **v.** 使恢復精神，使消除疲勞

100. take over　接替⋯，接手⋯

例　She'll take over the cooking while her mother goes shopping.

註　take through 向⋯詳細解釋⋯ ／ take up 開始從事；開始養成⋯習慣

101. take place　發生

例　I don't know exactly what took place in the lobby.

註　exactly **adv.** 全然，完全 ／ lobby **n.** 大廳

102. **to your heart's content**　盡情地，盡興地

例 This lunch is my treat and you can eat and drink to your heart's content.

註 treat *n.* 招待，款待／content *n.* 心滿意足，幸福

103. **try on**　試穿…

例 Why didn't she try on this lovely dress?

註 try out 試用，試驗／try out for 爭取參加；參加…選拔

T

104. **turn ~ around**　好轉

例 The $300 thousand loan will help turn his factory's finances around.

註 finances *n.* 經濟狀況，財務狀況／turn out 結果為…，發展成…

105. **turn down**　拒絕…

例 I'll have to turn down your offer flat!

註 turn to 開始做…／offer *n.* 建議，提議／flat *adv.* 完全地，徹底地

106. **turn off**　關閉…

例 When exiting the office, please turn off your computer.

註 exit *v.* 離開；退出(電腦程式)／turn on 打開，開啟

107. **turn up**　（意外地）發現

例 The lost documents finally turned up in a corner of his office.

註 document *n.* 文件／corner *n.* 角落／cut corners 草草行事，偷工減料

108. up to　由…決定，有責任…

例 It's up to all of you to solve the trouble.

註 solve *v.* 解決 ／ solution *n.* 解決方法 ／ trouble *n.* 問題；煩惱

109. wait for　等待…

例 Don't be late and your breakfast is waiting for you.

註 wait out 等(壞事)結束 ／ wait up 熬夜等待

U
W

New TOEIC 多益測驗常出現的
Phrases 片語

001. additional charge 額外收費

註 additional **a.** 附加的，額外的 ／ in addition to~ 除了…之外

002. annual report 年度報告

註 annual **a.** 每年的，一年一次的 ／ annuity **n.** 年金，養老金；養老保險

003. automated teller machine 自動提款機，ATM

註 automated **a.** 自動化的 ／ teller **n.** (銀行)出納員；計票員

004. baggage claim 行李提領處

註 baggage = luggage 行李 ／ claim **n.** 主張，聲稱；索取

005. branch office 分公司，辦事處，分支機構

註 branch out 開拓新業務；創業 ／ branch **n.** 分支機構；分支；支流

006. company picnic 公司野餐會

註 no picnic 不輕鬆，不愉快 → It's no picnic to live in a romote place.

007. convenience store 便利商店

註 convenient **a.** 方便的，近便的 ／ convenience food (只需加熱的)方便食品

008. courtesy bus 免費接駁車

註 courtesy **a.** 免費提供的 ／ courtesy call 禮貌性拜訪(問候電話)

009. **financial statements**　財務報表

註　finances　*n.* 財務狀況　／　joint statement　聯合聲明

010. **fiscal year = financial year**　會計年度

註　fiscal　*a.* 財務的；金融的　／　financial adviser　財務顧問

011. **flight attendant**　空服員

註　car park attendant 停車場服務員　／　cabin crew (飛機)座艙服務員

012. **gift shop**　禮品店

註　gifted = talented　*a.* 有天賦的　／　gift voucher 禮券　= gift token

013. **grocery store**　食品雜貨店

註　groceries　*n.* 食品雜貨　／　grocer　*n.* 食品雜貨商

014. **health certificate**　健康證明(書)

註　health club　健身俱樂部　／　fitness center 健身中心

015. **interest rate**　利率

註　interest　*n.* 利息　／　interest group　利益團體

016. **limited edition**　限量版

註　limited　*a.* 有限度的，受限制的　／　limitless　*a.* 無限的，無限度的

017. **maintenance department**　維修部門

註　regular maintenance 定期保養　／　routine maintenance 日常保養

018. **market share** 市場佔有率

註 market research 市場調查 ／ shareholder **n.** 股東

019. **parking lot** 停車場

註 parking space 停車位 ／ parking ticket 違規停車罰單

020. **personnel change** 人事變更，人事異動

註 personnel **n.** 全體人員；人力資源部

021. **physical examination** 身體檢查，體檢

註 physical appearance 外貌 ／ under examination 在審查中

022. **prior engagement** 有約在先

註 = prior arrangement ／ prior **a.** 先前的 ／ prior to～ 先在…之前

023. **product sheet** 產品說明書

註 product placement 置入性廣告

024. **production line** 生產線，裝配線

註 = assembly line ／ productivity **n.** 生產力(率)

025. **real estate** 房地產，不動產

註 realtor = estate agent 房地產經紀人 ／ estate **n.** 住宅區

026. **sales campaign** 銷售活動

註 sales force 銷售團隊 ／ sales pitch 商品宣傳 ／ publicity campaign 宣傳活動

027. **savings account** 儲蓄帳戶

註 savings *n.* 存款，節餘 ／ energy-saving *a.* 節約能源的

028. **shopping mall** 購物中心

註 shopping cart = shopping trolley 購物推車 ／ mall *n.* 購物商場中心

029. **staff meeting** 員工會議

註 full-time sataff 全職人員 ／ staff shortage 人手不足

030. **stock market** 股市

註 stocktaking *n.* 盤點，清點存貨 ／ stock *n.* 股票；(商店)庫存貨

031. **vending machine** 自動販賣機

註 vendor *n.* 小販，攤販 ／ pedlar *n.* 流動小販

New TOEIC 聽力測驗常出現的
Homonyms 同音異義字

01 air , heir — 發音皆為 / ɛr /

> air *n.* 空氣；on (the) air 播出；*v.* 播放，播出
> heir *n.* 繼承人（者）；heiress *n.* 女繼承人

02 altar , alter — 發音皆為 / ˋɔltɚ /

> altar *n.* （教堂的）祭壇
> alter *v.* 改變；變化；修改（衣服）

03 bare , bear — 發音皆為 / bɛr /

> bare *a.* 露出的；空的，光禿禿的；僅有的
> bear *n.* 熊；*v.* 忍耐，容忍；具有；運送；出產，生產；bear out 證實，為…作
> 證

04 berry , bury — 發音皆為 / ˋbɛri /

> berry *n.* 漿果
> bury *v.* 埋葬，掩埋；bury oneself in ~ 專心於…，沉浸於…

05 bough , bow — 發音皆為 / baʊ /

> bough *n.* 粗（大）樹枝
> bow *n.* 弓；鞠躬；*v.* 鞠躬，低頭；bow out 退出，辭職

06 brake , break — 發音皆為 / brek /

> brake *n./v.* 煞車；brake hard (sharply) 緊急煞車
> break *n.* 休息；好運，良機；break down 故障，損壞；break out 爆發，發生

07 cell , sell — 發音皆為 / sɛl /

cell *n.* 細胞；基層團體；電池；cellphone 手機
sell *v.* 賣，出售；sell off 廉價出售；sell on 轉賣；sell out 售完，賣光；sell-by date（食品）銷售期限

08 cite , sight , site — 發音皆為 / saɪt /

cite *v.* 舉出；引用，引證
sight *n.* 視力；景觀；in (within) sight 看得見；in one's sight 在…看來；out of sight，out of mind 眼不見，心不想
site *n.* 地點，場所；campsite 營地(區)

09 complement , compliment
— 發音皆為 / ˈkɑmpləˌmɛnt /

complement *v.* 與…互補；補充；full complement 足額
compliment *v.* 讚美，稱讚；complimentary *a.* 免費的

10 council , counsel — 發音皆為 / ˈkaʊnsḷ /

council *n.*（地方）議會；委員會；council chamber 會議室
counsel *v.* 諮詢與輔導；建議；*n.* 律師；忠告

11 dear , deer — 發音皆為 / dɪr /

dear *adv.* 付出代價；cost ~ dear 使…損失慘重
deer *n.* 鹿

12 desert , dessert — 發音皆為 / dɪˈzɜt /

desert / dɪˈzɜt /　*v.* 拋棄，脫離
　　　　/ ˈdɛzət /　*n.* 沙漠；枯燥乏味的地方
dessert *n.* 甜點；pudding *n.*（英）甜點，甜食

13 dew , due — 發音皆為 / du /

dew *n.* 露珠（水）；dewdrop *n.* 露珠
due *a.* 預定的；預產期的；due date 期限，預定日期

14 fair , fare — 發音皆為 / fɛr /

fair *n.* 商品展覽（交易）會；園遊會；義賣會；*a.* 公平的；尚可的
fare *n.* 車（船、機）費；菜餚，食物

15 flour , flower — 發音皆為 / flaur /

flour *n.* 粉，麵粉
flower *n./v.* 開花；flower arranging 插花

16 hair , hare — 發音皆為 / hɛr /

hair *n.* 頭髮；not turn a hair 面不改色，毫不驚慌
hare *n.* 野兔；hare-brained *a.* 愚蠢的

17 heal , heel — 發音皆為 / hil /

heal *v.* 治癒；康復；heal a breach 消除分歧（裂痕）
heel *n.* 腳後跟；at one's heels 緊跟在…後面

18 hole , whole — 發音皆為 / hol /

hole *n.* 洞，孔；in a hole 在困境中
whole *n.* 整體，整個；as the whole 整體看來，總體上；on the whole 總而言之

19 knight , night — 發音皆為 / naɪt /

knight *n.* 騎士
night *n.* 夜晚；call it a night 收工，今晚到此結束

20 **mail , male** — 發音皆為 / mel /

mail　*v.* 郵寄；mail out 大宗郵寄
male　*n./a.* 男（雄）性（的）

21 **morning , mourning** — 發音皆為 / ˋmɔrnɪŋ /

morning　*n.* 早晨
mourning　*n.* 追悼儀式；悼念；mournful *a.* 悲痛的

22 **pail , pale** — 發音皆為 / pel /

pail　*n.* （水）桶
pale　*a.* 淺的，淡的；蒼白的

23 **pray , prey** — 發音皆為 / pre /

pray　*v.* 祈禱；pray for 祈禱，渴望
prey　*n.* 獵物；*v.* 捕捉；prey on (upon) 欺負；捕食

24 **raise , raze** — 發音皆為 / rez /

raise　*n.* 加薪；*v.* 抬起；增加；引起
raze　*v.* 徹底摧毀；夷為平地

25 **reign , rein** — 發音皆為 / ren /

reign　*n.* 統治（支配）時期；*v.* 統治，支配，盛行
rein　*n.* 控制（權）；*v.* 控制；rein in (back) 控制，限制

26 **right , rite , write** — 發音皆為 / raɪt /

right　*n.* 對，右邊；*a.* 對的；*adv.* 正好，正確地；by rights 按理說
rite　*n.* 儀式，典禮；funeral rite 葬禮
write　*v.* 寫；write away for , write off for 寫信詢問（索取）

27 **role , roll** — 發音皆為 / rol /

role **n.** 角色；play ~ role 扮演…角色
roll **v.** 滾動；ready to roll 準備就緒

28 **sail , sale** — 發音皆為 / sel /

sail **v.** 航行；sail through ~ 順利通過 …
sale **n.** 出售；sales 銷售量（額）；for sale 待售；on sale = on offer 降價出售

29 **seam , seem** — 發音皆為 / sim /

seam **n.** 接縫，接口；come (fall) apart at the seams 解體，癱瘓
seem **v.** 看來；似乎；seemingly **adv.** 看起來，表面上

30 **sew , so , sow** — 發音皆為 / so /

sew **v.** 縫補；get (have) ~(all) sewn up 順利完成（解決）…
so **adv./conj.** 那麼；因此，所以
sow **v.** 播(種)，散播

31 **sole , soul** — 發音皆為 / sol /

sole **n.** 鞋底，腳底 **a.** 唯一的，僅有的
soul **n.** 心靈；靈魂；精神

32 **some , sum** — 發音皆為 / sʌm /

some / səm , sʌm / 一些，某些
sum **n.** 金額；總數；**v.** 總結；概括；sum up 總括

33 **stair , stare** 發音皆為 / stɛr /

stair **n.** 樓梯；staircase **n.** （包括扶手的）樓梯
stare **v.** 注視，盯著看

34 **steal , steel** — 發音皆為 / stil /

steal　*n.* 極便宜的東西；*v.* 偷竊
steel　*n.* 鋼（鐵）

35 **tail , tale** — 發音皆為 / tel /

tail　*n.* 尾巴；*v.* 盯哨
tale　*n.* （虛構的）故事；a tale of woe 傷心事

36 **wait , weight** — 發音皆為 / wet /

wait　　*n.* 等待的時間；*v.* 等待；wait around (about) 乾等（耗）著
weight　*n.* 重量；重物；負擔

37 **ware , wear** — 發音皆為 / wɛr /

ware　*n.* 陶（瓷）器；wares 商品，貨物
wear　*n.* 服裝；磨損，損耗；*v.* 穿著；磨損；wear out 使精疲力竭，用壞

38 **way , weigh** — 發音皆為 / we /

way　　*n.* 方法；道路；have a way with ～ 專門能對付…，與…有特殊關係
weigh　*v.* 秤重量；weigh on 使沮喪（煩惱）

39 **weak , week** — 發音皆為 / wik /

weak　*a.* （虛）弱的，差的
week　*n.* 星期，週；week in and week out 接連好多星期

New TOEIC 聽力測驗常出現的
Similar Words 相似字

accede	v.	同意，應允；就職，就任(總統)
exceed	v.	超過，超出

adapt	v.	適應；修改；adaption = adaptation *n.* 改編(版)本，適應
adopt	v.	採用，採納；收養；領養；adopted son 養子；adoptive parents 養父母

affect	v.	影響；假裝；affected manner 做作的舉止
effect	n.	影響；效果 v. 達到…效果，使產生；come into effect 開始實施(生效)

assure	v.	確保，使確信；assured a. 有把握的，肯定的；assured reply 肯定的回覆
ensure	v.	保證，擔保
insure	v.	給…保險；the insured 被保險人

climactic	a.	(事情、時刻等) 非常令興奮；高潮的；climax n. (事件、情勢)高潮
climatic	a.	氣候的；climate n. 氣候

continual	a.	從不間斷的，頻頻的；continual arguing 不斷的爭吵
continuous	a.	連續不斷的，接連的；continuous pressure 持續不斷的壓力

credible	a.	可信的，可靠的；有實力的；credible witness 可靠的證人；credible opponent 有實力的對手
creditable	a.	值得讚揚的，令人欽佩的；creditable performance 值得讚揚的表現

decent	*a.*	好的，像樣的；寬容的；恰當的；decent chance 好機會；decent thing 恰當的事
descent	*n.*	下降；世系；ascent *n.* 上升

disinterested	*a.*	不偏頗的，公正的；disinterested witness and observer 公正的證人和目擊者
uninterested	*a.*	不感興趣的，冷漠的
uninteresting	*a.*	無趣的，乏味的

dual	*a.*	雙的，雙重的；dual nationality 雙重國籍
duel	*n.*	競爭，較量；爭論；a duel of words 論戰，口頭爭論

economic	*a.*	經濟的；省錢的；economic policy 經濟政策；economic way 省錢（經濟）的方式；economic benefits 經濟效益
economical	*a.*	節儉的；低價的，便宜的；economical substitute 低價替代品

effective	*a.*	有效的；實際的；effective communication 有效的溝通（交流）；effective control 實際上（有效的）控制
efficient	*a.*	效率高的；efficient machine 效率高的機器

eminent	*a.*	傑出的，著名的
imminent	*a.*	即將發生的，迫近的；imminent danger 瀕臨的危險

extant	*a.*	尚存的，現存的
extinct	*a.*	絕種的，消失的，不復存在的

historic	*a.*	歷史上著名的（場所）；有歷史意義的；historic city 歷史名城
historical	*a.*	與歷史有關的；史學的；historical event 歷史事件；historical research 史學研究

imaginable	a.	想像得到的；imaginable situation 想像得到的情況
imaginary	a.	假想的，想像中的；imaginary rival 假想的對手；imaginary enemy 假想敵
imaginative	a.	有創造力的，有創意的，虛構的；imaginative solution 有創意的解決方法；imaginative writing 虛構的作品
incredible	a.	令人驚訝的，了不起的；難以置信的；incredible performance 了不起的表演
incredulous	a.	不能相信的；表示懷疑的；不輕信的
ingenious	a.	新奇的，別出心裁的；ingenious device 新奇的器具
ingenuous	a.	天真的，單純的
luxuriant	a.	（植物）茂盛的；濃密的；luxuriant plants 茂盛的植物；luxuriant hair 濃密的頭髮
luxurious	a.	豪華的；luxurious hotel 豪華的旅館
marital	a.	婚姻的；marital problem 婚姻問題
martial	a.	戰爭的；好戰的；martial low 戒嚴法，軍事管制
moral	n.	道德（規範）；moral support 精神（道義）支持
morale	n.	士氣
mortal	a.	致命的；mortal wound 致命的創傷
official	a.	正式的，官方的；official representative 官方代表
officious	a.	好用權威的，雞毛當令箭的；officious guard 好用權威的警衛
personal	a.	私人的，隱私的；personal matter 隱私
personnel	n.	員工；人力資源部；全體人員

practicable	*a.*	可行的，能實行的；practicable system 可行的制度
practical	*a.*	實際的；實用的；確實可行的；practical experience 實務

precede	*v.*	先於…，在…之前；比…更重要
proceed	*v.*	持續，繼續發生（進行）；前往

principal	*n.*	校長；主角；本金　*a.* 主要的，首要的；principal aim 主要目標
principle	*n.*	原理，原則；guiding principle 指導原則

respectable	*a.*	可敬的；體面的；respectable life 體面的生活
respectful	*a.*	恭敬的，表示尊敬的
respective	*a.*	各自的，分別的；respective decision 各自的決定

sensible	*a.*	合理的；切合實際的，實用的；了解的；理智的；sensible person 理智的人
sensitive	*a.*	敏感的；靈敏的；多愁善感的；小心謹慎的；sensitive instrument 靈敏的儀器

stationary	*a.*	靜止的，不動的；stationary vehicle 停止不動的車輛
stationery	*a.*	文具；stationer *n.* 文具商

statue	*n.*	雕像，塑像
stature	*n.*	身高；聲望
status	*n.*	身份；社會地位；狀況，情形
statute	*n.*	法令，規章；章程

New TOEIC *WORD LIST*
最新單字表

撰文 / 高志豪

accept receive ; approve	**anniversary**
v. 同意，贊同；接受	*n.* 紀念日；週年紀念
accommodation	**announcement** declaration
n. 住處；公寓；工作場所	*n.* 宣告；公告；啟事
account	**annual** yearly
n. 銀行帳戶；帳目	*a.* 一年一次的；年度的
address speak	**apparently**
v. 向…演講(發言、講話)；稱呼	*adv.* 顯然；據說；似乎
adjust regulate	**applaud** praise
v. 調整；適應	*v.* 稱讚；鼓掌
advertisement	**appliance**
n. 廣告；宣傳	*n.* 家用電器
affect influence ; pretend	**apply** put to practical use
v. 影響；假裝	*v.* 申請；應用；適用
allow permit ; provide	**appointment**
v. 允許，准許；給予	*n.* 約會，會面；委派，任命
altitude height	**appreciate** esteem
n. 海拔高度	*v.* 欣賞；感激；增值；意識；明白
ambulance	**approachable**
n. 救護車	*a.* 易親近的；可到達的

appropriately properly

adv. 合適地；恰當地

approve

v. 贊同；認可；核准

argument debate, arguing

n. 爭論，爭吵；論點

arrange classify

v. 安排；籌備；整理

assign appoint；allot

v. 指派；分配

assignment

n. 作業；分派的任務；指派

attach join；connect

v. 附上；連接；附屬於

attend take care of

v. 參加，出席；照料，看護

attention notice or observation

n. 注意(力)；關照

audience

n. 觀眾，聽眾

available handy

a. 可獲得的；現成的

avoid keep away from

v. 避免；防止

B

baggage luggage

n. 行李；(英) luggage

beverage drinks

n. 飲料

bid a bidding

n. 投標；報價；努力

blame condemn

v. 責備；歸咎於

board

n. 董事會；委員會；佈告板

book

v. 預定；做…筆錄

borrow

v. 借入；借用

brochure pamphlet

n. 小冊子

browse

v. 搜尋(資料)；隨意瀏覽

budget

n. 預算(額)

bulletin

n. 公告；佈告；會刊

cancel abolish
v. 取消；廢除，終止

candidate
n. 候選人；求職者；考生

cart = shopping trolley
n. 購物手推車；手推車 = trolley

celebrate
v. 慶祝；讚揚

chat talk informally
v. 閒聊，聊天

checkup medical examination
n. 體檢；檢查

chop mince
v. 切碎；劈開；削減

circle move around
v. 盤旋；環繞，圍繞

clearance
n. 清除；(官方)許可；(支票)兌現

client a customer
n. 顧客，客戶；委託人；病人

colleague coworker
n. 同事；同行

column
n. 柱，欄；專欄

complaint complaining
n. 投訴

complete finish
v. 完成；結束

computerize
v. 電腦化

conduct lead ; direct
v. 進行；引導

conference
n. 會議；會談

confirm make firm
v. 證實；確認

confusing bewildering
a. 令人迷惑的；混亂的

contractor
n. 承包商，承包人

convenient handy
a. 方便的，近便的

convertible
a. 可轉變（換）的

corporation
n. 公司；法人（團體）

cover include

v. 蓋；包括；報導

crowd cram

v. 使擁擠；聚集

deadline

n. 最後期限；截止日期

definitely certainly

adv. 確切地，毫無疑問地

delay postpone；detain

v. 延續；延期

demonstrate

v. 證明；示威

deposit

v. 留下；存，存入

descend slope downward

v. 下降，下來；降臨

destination

n. 目的地

device

n. 設備；器具；方法

diagram

n. 示意圖；圖表

directly straight；instantly

adv. 直接地；坦率地；立即

disconnect separate

v. 切斷；斷線

discount disregard

v. 降價；打折扣；不重視

division segment；department

n. 部門；分配；分歧；差距

dock

n. 碼頭；船塢

document

n. 文件；公文

double duplicate

v. 加倍；增加一倍

downsizing

n. 縮編；編小規模

draft

n. 草稿；草案

drink

v. 喝，飲 n. 飲料，酒

driveway

n. （屋前的）車道

duty

n. 稅，關稅；責任，義務

efficiency

n. 效率;效能

election

n. 選舉

entire whole , complete

a. 全部的;整個的

estimate calculate

v. 估計,估算

examine investigate

v. 仔細研究(審查);仔細檢查

exceed surpass

v. 超過,超出

exchange interchange

v. 交換;兌換;調換

executive

n. 高層主管;行政部門

expect

v. 預料,預計;期盼

expense financial cost

n. 花費;費用

expensive costly

a. 昂貴的;代價高的

experience

n. 經驗;經歷

experiment test

n. 實驗,試驗

expert specialist

n. 專家;行家

expire come to an end

v. 到期;結束

extend stretch out ; expand

v. 延伸;擴大;加長

extension extent

n. 延長(部份、期限);擴張

fabric framework ; structure

n. 織物,布料;結構,組織

facility

n. 裝置;設施;場所

feature

n. 特點,特色;專題報導(節目)

feed

v. 餵養,飼養 n. 飼料,化學肥料

field

n. 領域,範圍;場

fix fasten ; repair

v. 安裝；修理；安排

float

v. 漂浮；閒蕩

flyer handbill

n. 廣告傳單

form shape ; kind

n. 形式；表格；形狀；種類

fraud deceit ; trickery

n. 詐欺；欺騙

funding

n. 基金；專款

fundraiser

n. 募款者；募款活動

gather accumulate

v. 聚集，收集；增加

gaze stare

v. 凝視，盯視

grip grasp securely

v. 緊抓(握)；強烈影響

guarantee promise

v. 保證；擔保

hang

v. 懸掛；吊死

headquarters

n. 總部；總公司；總辦事處

hire

v. 租用；僱用

hold possess ; occupy

v. 舉辦；保有；持有；握著

identical exactly alike

a. 完全相同的，一模一樣的

inconvenience

n. 不方便，不便之處

increase

v. 增加，增長

incredible unbelievable

a. 難以置信的；不可思議的

inform

v. 通知，告知

information

n. 資訊，資料；消息

inspect look at carefully

v. 檢查，檢驗

instrument

n. 儀器，工具；樂器

investment

n. 投資（額）

invitation inviting

n. 邀請；請柬

invoice

n. 發票；發貨清單

issue

n. 議題，問題；（期刊）期；發行

laboratory

n. 實驗室

labor-cost

n. 勞力成本

lamppost

n. 路燈柱

land

v. 到達；降落；把…送到…

layoff unemployment

n. 解僱；停止工作（出賽）

layover

n. 中途停留

lean rely on (upon)

v. 俯身；倚靠；斜靠

lease

n. 租約；活力；煥然一新

letterhead

n. 信箋抬頭

light

a. 輕的，輕柔的；少量的

limit

n. 限制；限度；限額

load

n. 載重物；工作量 *v.* 負荷，裝貨

locate

v. 找出；坐落於

management

n. 經營，管理

manual handy book

n. 手冊，說明書；操作指南

medication medicine

n. 藥；藥物

merchandise

n. 商品　**v.** 推銷

negotiation

n. 談判，協商

nervous　animated

a. 緊張的；害怕的；易激動的

nomination

n. 提名（作品）

notice

n. 佈告，公告，啟事　**v.** 注意到

notify　inform

v. 通知；報告

observe　notice ; remark

v. 觀察；注意；評論

occupational

a. 職業的

occur　happen ; take place

v. 發生

opening　beginning

a. 開始的，首先的

operate　act ; manage

v. 運轉；營運；操作

order

n. 訂單，訂貨

originate　begin ; start

v. 開源；開始；創始

overlook　ignore ; supervise

n. 忽視（略）；俯瞰

oversee　supervise

v. 監督；管理

overstaffed

a. 超員的，人員過多的

overtime

n. 加班　**adv.** 非常活躍

pack

v. 打包；擠滿；包著

package

n. 包裹；整套方案（措施）

passenger

n. 乘客；旅客

pave

v. 舖設，舖

paycheck payment

n. 薪水，工資

permission consent

n. 許可；容許

photocopy

n./v. 複印；影印

place

v. 放置，施加　n. 地方，位置，席位

plant factory

n. 工廠；植物

policy

n. 政策；方針

post

v. 郵寄；張貼

postpone delay

v. 延緩；延遲

pour emit；utter

v. 傾倒；湧出

predict foretell

v. 預測；預言

preparation

n. 準備，預備；籌備工作

presentation

n. 報告；展示；表演

procedure

n. 手續；程序

process

n. 過程；步驟

product result；outgrowth

n. 產物，產品；結果

profit advantage；gain

n. 利益，利潤；好處

progress development

n. 進行；進展　v. 前進

prohibit prevent；hinder

v. 禁止；阻止

project proposal

n. 計劃　v. 預計，投影

promotion

n. 晉升；宣傳；推銷

proposal

n. 計劃；建議；求婚

provide supply

v. 提供；供應，供給

public

n. 民眾，公眾　a. 公共的，公開的

publish issue；announce

v. 出版；發行，發表

purchase buy

v. 購買，採購

quarter

n. 四分之一；地區

raise lift ; increase

v. 舉起；增加；提高

reasonably sensibly

adv. 相當地；理性地

receipt

n. 收據；receipts 進帳，收入

receive

v. 收到；接受；接待

recently newly

adv. 近來；最近

reception

n. 接待處；招待會；歡迎會

recession depression

n. 經濟衰退（不景氣）

recognize

v. 認出；承認；表揚

recommend suggest

v. 建議；推薦；介紹

reduce lessen

v. 減少，降低

reduced

a. 減少的，降低（價）的

reference

n. 提及；參閱；介紹人（信）

refund repayment

n. 退款

reimburse pay back

v. 償還；核銷

release set free ; issue

v. 釋放；發佈；發行

reliable dependable

a. 可靠的，可信賴的

relocate

v. 重新安置；搬遷

remind

v. 提醒；使想起

renew revive

v. 重新開始；再度…

renewable

a. 可延期的；可再生的

renovate restore

v. 修復，裝修；翻新（建物）

repair fix；renew

v. 修理，修補；補救

replacement

n. 更換；代替的人（物）

reputation fame

n. 名聲；知名度

require need；demand

v. 需要；要求；規定

researcher

n. 研究人員

reservation

n. 預訂

resolve solve；determine

v. 解決；決定，下決心

response reaction；reply

n. 反應；答案

responsibility

n. 責任；職責

responsible reliable

a. 負責任的；可靠的

retire

v. 退休；退出；更換

revenue income

n. 收入；營收

revised amended

a. 修正過的

row quarrel

n. 爭吵，吵鬧；一排（行）

saving

n. 節餘，節省的量

savings

n. 存款，儲蓄金

scatter sprinkle；disperse

v. 散播；使分散

schedule

n. 日程表，計劃表，時間表 *v.* 排定

seat

v. 使坐下，容納 *n.* 座位，席位

shareholder

n. 股東

shelf

n. 架子，貨架

shield

n. 防護物；盾牌

ship

v. 運送；託運

shipment

n. 運輸，運載；一批貨物

shipyard

n. 船塢；造船廠

sip drink a little at a time

v. 啜飲；小口地喝

slight small; slender

a. 些微的，少量的；纖弱的

spare extra; free

a. 備用的；多餘的

specification

n. 明細；規格；計劃書

split disunite; separate

v. 分開；劃分

stack

v. 堆放，堆滿

staircase

n. （有扶手的）樓梯

stare gaze steadily

v. 注視；盯著看

stick pierce; attach

v. 插入；黏貼

stock

n. 儲備（物）；庫存貨；股票（份）

strike walkout

n. 罷工；一擊

subscription

n. 訂閱，訂購；訂閱費

suggestion hint

n. 提議；暗示；可能性

suitable appropriate

a. 適合的，適宜的

summon call together

v. 傳喚；請求；召開（會議）

supervisor

n. 監督者，督導者

supply stock

n. 供給量；supplies 日常用品

surgical

a. 外科手術的；外科的

suspend stop; hang

v. 暫停，中止；懸掛

switch shift; change

v. 轉換；替換；調班

symmetrical

a. 對稱的

T

tear disrupt

v. 撕碎（破），撕毀

tenant

n. 房客；承租人

tilt incline

v. 傾斜；影響

transfer convey

v. 移轉；轉乘；調動

trim

v. 修剪，削減

trustee

n. 受託人；託管人（機構）

type

n. 類型 *v.* 打（字）

U

unbelievable incredible

a. 難以相信的，不可思議的

unoccupied

a. 無人佔用的；空著的

unroll display ; open

v. 舖開；展開

update

v. 更新 *n.* 最新消息，更新軟體

V

vacancy empty space

n. 空缺；空房

vehicle

n. 交通工具；車輛

W

wait

v. 等待；盼望

warehouse

n. 倉庫；貨倉

warranty

n. 保證書；保固單

wave

v. 揮（手），招（手）；搖擺

welcome

v. 歡迎，迎接

wonder doubt

v. 疑惑；納悶

多益單字 DNA

撰文／　高志豪

Part I　Eats, Shoots & Leaves?

　　The Sunday Times（週日泰晤士報）專欄作家、書評家兼 BBC Radio 4 （英國國家廣播公司四號電台）的節目製作人 —— Lynne Truss 女士，寫了一本很「奇怪」的暢銷書。的確奇怪！因為它是一本教人正確使用標點符號的書，這種書居然能暢銷，實在不可思議！不過，這確實是難得一見的好書，值得想讓英文能力更上層樓的人買來看！

　　筆者就從這本書的書名談起 —— Eats, Shoots & Leaves。這是一則有關標點符號的笑話：一隻熊貓走進餐廳，點了一份簡餐，吃完之後，牠掏出槍來，對空開了幾槍，不付帳就要離開。在踏出大門之前，牠丟給服務生一本「野生動物手冊」，微笑著說：「別怕！你查一下手冊裡面 Panda（熊貓）那一欄！」服務生查閱之下，發現手冊上寫著：A panda eats, shoots and leaves.（熊貓吃東西，開槍，然後離開。）原來是誤植了一個逗號，原句應為 A panda eats shoots and leaves.（熊貓吃嫩芽和樹葉）。因為多了一個標點符號，整個意思就完全扭曲了。

　　我們初學英文的時候，都記 shoot 是「開槍」、leave 是「離開」之意，但是在 "A panda eats shoots and leaves." 句中，兩字都當名詞，shoots 是「嫩芽、嫩苗」，而 leaves 則指「樹葉」（leaf 的複數形）。其實它們的用法還有很多，舉一些例子吧 ——

> Her novel has **shot** straight to the champion of the bestseller list.
> 她的小說頓時躍居暢銷書排行榜的冠軍。
> The world premiere of her latest film **shot** her to stardom overnight.
> 她的新片在世界各地的首映，使她一夜成名。

　　shoot 是「突然迅速發生」的意思；shoot 也可當作「突然提出、發出」解釋，例如 ——

> Reporters were **shoot**ing questions at our company's spokesperson in the press conference.
> 在記者會中，記者們向我們公司發言人連續發問。

新｜版｜多｜益｜測｜驗｜解｜析

至於 leaves ，樹葉的單數形是 leaf，leaf 又可以是動詞，作「匆匆翻閱」解，例如 ——

> She was absent-minded and sat **leaf**ing through a gossip magazine.
> 她心不在焉，只是坐著隨手翻閱一本八卦雜誌。

leaf 可以指「一頁」，如 one of the leaves of her novel 她小說中的一頁，a leaf of paper 一頁紙。leaf 加上字尾 **-let**（小），變成了 leaflet 「小葉子、傳單」；leaflet 又可以當作動詞「散發傳單」。leaf 如果加上 **-y**（形容詞字尾），就變成 leafy，則是「多葉的，多樹木的」。

再回頭談 leaves 這個字，它去掉 s 之後，變成 leave 「離開」；leave 如果作為名詞，是「假期、休假」的意思。例如 ——

> annual leave 年假   sick leave 病假
> maternity leave 產假   parental leave 育嬰假
> personal leave 事假   compassionate leave 喪假
> unpaid leave 留職停薪、無薪假期

> I met an old friend while I was on **leave**.
> 我休假時，碰到了一個老朋友。(這可真難得吧！)

掰了這許多，筆者無非是要提醒各位：英文裡頭最簡單的單字，卻是最常用、最實用，也最管用。一味地記一些少用罕見的單字，只是自討苦吃；因為記了就忘，忘了再記，終歸還是忘記，最後只能徒呼負負了！

Part II   **Passive Smoking !**

再看看以下 *TOEIC* 經常出現的簡單片語 ——

behind schedule / time 比預定時間晚

例 The express train arrived behind schedule.
快車比預定的時間還晚抵達。

ahead of schedule / time 提前

例 The reception for the new president ended ahead of schedule.
新任總經理的歡迎會提前結束了。

on schedule / time　準時

例　The project was completed on schedule.　計劃如期完成。

　　至於 according to schedule，是「照預定時間…」，而 busy schedule、full schedule 就是「行程滿檔」，tight schedule 則是「行程緊湊」。

　　再多學幾個 **TOEIC** 測驗中常出現的片語吧 ——

come into effect　開始實施(生效)

例　The tax increase came into effect on New Year's Day. 增稅案從元旦開始生效。

come up with　想出，提出

例　Is that the novel solution he came up with? 那是他想出來的新解決方法嗎?

　　novel = new，在這裡是「新的，新奇的」之意，而 solution 是「解決方法」，原本還有「解答，答案，溶液」的意思。

to your heart's content　盡情地，盡興地

例　This lunch is my treat and you can eat and drink to your heart's content.
　　午餐算我請，你可以盡情地吃喝。

　　treat 當動詞是「對待，款待」，當名詞是「請客，作東」之意；I'd like this coffee to be my treat. (這咖啡我請客。)

be allergic to　對…極反感，過敏的

例　He is allergic to passive smoking.　他很討厭吸二手煙。

　　一般人誤以為吸二手煙是 smoking in second hand，這是「用二手吸煙」或「用秒針吸煙」的意思(second hand　秒針)；至於 second-hand books 則是「二手書」，a used car 是「中古車」。因為吸二手煙並非主動 (active) 去吸，而是被動的，所以用 passive。allergic 本來是「過敏的」，如 I'm allergic to flowers. 我對花過敏。allergic 又可引申為「對…極反感/討厭的」。

on duty　值勤(班)

例　He fell asleep while on duty.　他值班時睡著了。

　　「值班」用 on duty，「下班、不值班」則是 off duty，而 on guard duty 就是「站崗」了。

　　以上這些都是很實用的單字、片語，讀者稍加用心，其實不難記憶!
　　同時，也別忽略了閱讀。任何語言的學習過程中，語彙的累積和語法觀念的形成固然重要，但是不可否認的，要讓所習得的語彙、語法根深蒂固於腦海中，配合大

　新|版|多|益|測|驗|解|析

量的閱讀文章是必要的。所以每次測驗中，**New TOEIC** 的閱讀部份都有20篇左右的短文；再加上聽力部分 Part 3 的10組對話內容，以及 Part 4 的10段簡短獨白。聽力的這兩部份猶如 book-on-tape 有聲書一樣，等於讓考生「聽」了20篇文章。這還能說語文的學習，閱讀不重要嗎？

那麼，就讓筆者來談談：如何配合單字的記憶，養成閱讀的習慣。

 Part III

Justice?

高中的時候，筆者最討厭英文教科書（讀本），卻偏好詩歌、散文、隨筆之類的文章，因為這種輕薄短小的作品，文章短，容易看完；文章短，生字也少些；同時言簡意賅，富思想、哲理；寓意深長，能發人深省。且讓讀者們欣賞一下底下這篇小品，看看人們所謂的 Justice（正義）──

> To steal a flower we call mean,
> To rob a field is chivalry;
> Who kills the body he must die,
> Who kills the spirit he goes free.

其中算得上是「生字」的，大概是 chivalry 騎士精神（風範），也可說是「俠義」。至於 go free 是「自由自在，逍遙自在」的意思；mean 在這兒作「卑鄙」解釋。這個字很重要，有好幾個常用的意思，也可衍生出很多常用字來 ──

> For most people, a red rose **mean**s love and romance.
> 對大多數人來說，紅玫瑰花代表愛情和浪漫。

mean是「意指，意味」的意思，也可以作「吝嗇的，小氣的」解 ──

> My boss was too **mean** to put air conditioner on.
> 我的老闆很吝嗇，不肯開冷氣。

mean 當形容詞的話，還可以是「平均的」意思，如：the mean yearly rainfall 平均年降雨量。此外，mean 衍生出來的語彙不少，如──

> means 手段、方法　　　　　　　meaning 意義、意思
> meaningful 意思清楚的、意味深長的　meaningless 無意義的、意思不明確的
> means test 收入狀況調查

這都是看完短文後，該作的筆記（可以參閱字典），應該不會花太多時間吧？因為這類小品文章短小，所以筆者也常將它們順手翻譯出來。現在姑且試譯前面那四句於下：

偷摘一朵花，我們說是卑鄙，
竊佔一片原野，卻說成俠義；
塗炭生靈的人必死，
戕賊心靈的，卻逍遙自在。

再看一篇小品，也順便翻譯成中文 ──

Yea, death and prison we mete out	誠然，我們以死亡和牢獄
To small offenders of the laws,	懲罰小罪犯，
While honor, wealth, and full respect	卻將榮耀、財富與全部的敬意
On greater pirates we bestow.	贈給江洋大盜。

這段文字的書寫正常排列應該是 ──
Yea, we mete out death and prison to small offenders of the laws while we bestow
honor, wealth, and full respect on greater pirates.

文中的 mete out 是「給予懲罰」的意思；offender是「罪犯」，原形動詞offend「犯罪、違反、冒犯」；bestow 「贈予、授予」；pirate 「海盜」，pirate books 就變成了「盜版書」。如此，在閱讀的過程中，除了從字典裡查閱文章中不認識的單字、片語之外，還應細細體會作者所撰內容的寓意，不應該只是大概看看，那只會留下浮光掠影的印象罷了。如果碰到自己覺得精彩的語句、出色的片段，還可以將它翻譯成中文。常常練習，自然能訓練出對英文語彙、語法的敏感度了。讀者們，您以為然否？

讀者們若能經常閱讀一些文章，由淺而深，由輕薄而厚重，養成閱讀的習慣，持之以恆，英文能力一定有長足的進步！尤其 *TOEIC* 測驗的範圍，只是測驗考生在職場、社交、生活三方面的英語能力，它不是商業英語，也不是專業領域的英語，則何懼之有？

NO MATERIAL ON THIS PAGE

CD 1   No. 5~8

Sample Test

New TOEIC

聽力測驗新題型新趨勢

撰文 / 高志豪
CD 1 | Tracks 5~8

　　ETS繼TOEFL iBT（托福網路化測驗）之後，又將TOEIC變臉、變裝，大大整修了一番；**New TOEIC** 新版多益已於2008年3月30日在台灣隆重登場（其實2006年5月早已在韓、日兩國實施了）。究竟TOEIC的新測驗新題型是舊瓶裝新酒、換湯不換藥？亦或是推陳出新、去蕪存菁，令人耳目一新？看倌們！且讓筆者試作聽力測驗的範例，細細道來——

Part I　Picture 圖片描述 / 第1-10題　 CD 1 No. 5

　　這一部份原本是考生最容易拿分的，卻被「腰斬」了；從原先舊題型的20道問題，刪減成只剩10題，但題型和測驗方式維持不變——試題本上只出現圖片，考生必須看圖、聽聲音、答題。

 Now listen to the four statements.

(A) The two people are tightrope walkers.
(B) The man on the left side is a street artist.
(C) The two men are playing "hide-and-seek".
(D) The man on the right side gambled away all his money.

（CD播出）聆聽四句話，並作答。

(A) 兩人是走鋼索的人。
(B) 左邊的男人是街頭藝術家。
(C) 兩個男人在玩「捉迷藏」。
(D) 右邊的男人輸光了所有的錢。

◎正答 ➡ **(B)**

・hide-and-seek 捉迷藏，躲貓貓(遊戲)　　・tightrope walker 走鋼索的人
・gamble away 賭輸掉，輸光

Part II Question-Response 應答問題 / 第11-40題

第二部份題數不變，仍維持30題，而題型和測驗方式依然不動如山——試題本上沒有任何圖片或文字內容，考生須聆聽一問三答的內容後，擇一正確的答案。

	（CD播出）
(Woman) How much is a taxi to the high speed rail station?	（女）搭計程車到高鐵車站，要多少錢？
(Man) (A) It takes thirty minutes. (B) Two hour's drive from here. (C) Eight dollars one way.	（男）(A) 要花30分鐘。 (B) 從這兒要兩個鐘頭的車程。 (C) 單程要八塊美金。

◎正答 ➡ **(C)**　　　・drive　*n.* 車程

 Part III Short Conversations 簡短對話 / 第41-70題

簡短對話這一部份從原先的一組三段對話，回答一個問題（共三十組對話，三十道問題），變成一組四段對話，回答三個問題，總計十組對話，三十道問題。同時，對話內容變長了一些，考生須仔細聆聽，必須聽懂大部份的對話內容（每組四段），才回答得出三個問題。

試作新試題範例如下——

Questions 41 through 43 refer to the following conversation.

(Woman) I heard you went to an American style Italian dinnerhouse. Can you tell me the name of it?

(Man) It's called The Blue Moonlight. It's gorgeous —— great food, traditional deco and classical music.

(Woman) That sounds good. I have some old friends coming in from New York next Friday and I'd like to take them somewhere special. How are the prices?

(Man) Oh, reasonable. I got a business card with its address and phone number on it. You can keep it.

🎧 根據以下的對話，回答第41~43題。

(女) 聽說你昨晚到一家美式義大利餐廳。能告訴我它的名字嗎？

(男) 它叫作「藍色月光」。這餐廳棒極了──有美食、復古裝潢和古典音樂演奏。

(女) 聽起來不錯！下個禮拜五，我有一些老朋友從紐約來，我想帶他們去一些特別的地方。它的收費如何？

(男) 價位很合理！我有一張它的名片，上面有地址、電話。你拿去好了！

· dinnerhouse **n.** 餐廳，晚宴餐廳
· reasonable **a.** 合理的
· gorgeous **a.** 極好的，非常漂亮的

41. What does the man give the woman?

    (A) An invitation card
    (B) A thank-you card
    (C) A business card
    (D) A toll-free number

41. 這男子給女子什麼東西？

    (A) 邀請卡
    (B) 感謝卡
    (C) 名片
    (D) 免付費電話

42. What are they talking about?

    (A) A restaurant
    (B) A resort
    (C) A party
    (D) Some buyers

42. 他們在談什麼？

    (A) 一家餐廳
    (B) 一個度假地
    (C) 一場舞會
    (D) 一些買家

43. What is the woman planning to do next?

    (A) Be on vacation
    (B) Take some friends out to eat
    (C) Go out on date with the man
    (D) Visit New York

43. 這女子之後打算做什麼？

    (A) 度假
    (B) 帶朋友去吃飯
    (C) 和這男子約會
    (D) 去紐約玩

◎正答 ➡ **41. (C)　42. (A)　43. (B)**

· toll-free number **n.** 免付費電話
· go out on date with ~　和~出去約會
· resort **n.** 度假地

原先第81~100題為Short Talks，新版多益自第71~100題為Short Talks；這一部份的題數從8~9篇簡短獨白，各出2~3道問題，演變成10篇，每篇出3道問題。筆者試作新試題範例如下——

Questions 71 through 73 refer to the following speech.

Thanks for inviting me to speak at your labor union. You've asked me to talk about what it's like being a police officer. Well, I'm going to be honest with you. It's a tough profession. I arrive at the office for work and have no idea what the day will bring. It could be a traffic accident, a murder or a false alarm. I rarely complete a holiday shift without having to report a suicide. It isn't easy. What kind of person measures up to such a job? Any one of you. You have to be a high school graduate and at least 20 years old to get into the Police Academy. First you have to pass a written exam. If you make it through that, you have to take a physical exam. Then you need a medical exam and get into the Police Academy for six months. If you are interested, get in touch with the Department of Personnel. Thanks a lot. And good luck !

感謝各位邀請我來你們的工會說幾句，你們要我談有關警察人員的事情。警察是很辛苦的行業！我一到辦公室就開始工作，而且不知道當天會發生什麼。可能是一件交通事故、一樁謀殺案或謊報。我很少過完輪休假期，而不須要報告一件自殺案件的。這工作不輕鬆。什麼樣的人適合這工作呢？你們任何一個都可以。必須高中畢業、年滿20歲，才可以進入警察學校。首先，你得先通過筆試。假使通過了，必須作體能測驗。然後再作健康檢查，同時進警察學校六個月。如果你們有興趣的話，和人事部門聯絡。謝謝！祝好運！

- labor union *n.* 工會
- holiday shift 輪休假期
- physical exam 體檢，體能（格）測驗
- false alarm 謊報
- suicide *n.* 自殺
- medical exam 健康（醫療）檢查

71. Who is the speaker probably addressing?

(A) members in police force
(B) high school graduates
(C) members of the trade union
(D) members of the Police Academy

71. 這演說者可能在向誰發表演說？

(A) 警察部門的成員
(B) 高中畢業生
(C) 工會的會員
(D) 警察學校學員

72. How are the speaker's holidays?

(A) He can complete the whole holiday.
(B) His holidays are always with incidents.
(C) He has no holiday shift.
(D) It's no picnic being a police officer.

72. 演講者的假期如何？

(A) 他能過完整個假期 。
(B) 他的假期總有不尋常的事故。
(C) 他沒有輪休假期。
(D) 擔任警察並不輕鬆。

73. What is the second exam you have to take if you want to be a police officer?

(A) medical exam
(B) written exam
(C) physical exam
(D) graduate exam

73. 假使你要當警察，你必須參加的第二項測驗是什麼？

(A) 健康檢查
(B) 筆試
(C) 體能測驗
(D) 畢業考

◎正答 ➡ **71. (C) 72. (B) 73. (C)**　　　　· trade union 工會

以上是TOEIC改變題型之後，新版多益聽力測驗的範例和簡單介紹，供作讀者們的參考。又許多讀者交相議論：TOEIC新試題新題型，是否使得多益測驗變得更難考了呢？筆者以為：不盡然。依照 ETS 全真試題看來，對原先實力在TOEIC 500分以下的考生，影響最大(變得較難)。但發表的官方版新版多益，因為聽力測驗滿分仍是 495 分，加上閱讀測驗 495 分，總分仍以 990 分計算。或許程度較好的考生對 *New TOEIC*的新考法會有些不適應，但是只要平常多作模擬測驗、多加練習，等「熟悉感」回來之後，自然可以回復應有的實力。又ETS台灣區代表忠欣公司已出版新版多益的新題型版本（筆者有幸主導此一官方版的ETS台灣區代表編輯委員會，參與製作、編譯工作），全球模考股份有限公司也推出**新版多益測驗指南**（New TOEIC Preparation Guide；18開，416頁，MP3+2CD，共2組完整試題）。

New TOEIC
閱讀測驗新題型新趨勢

　　New TOEIC 的 Reading Comprehension 部份，有較大的改變。今說明 *New TOEIC* 的閱讀部份新題型改變如下：

一、Part 5 **填空**：

　　共40題（第101題~140題），承襲原來的考法，毫無變動，連題數都一樣。

二、Part 6 **短文克漏字**：

　　共12題（第141題~152題），三到四篇短文章，每篇文章有四或三個空格（4 題或3題），必須從每題下面 (A)(B)(C)(D) 四個答案中，擇一正確答案。至於原先的Error Recognition（挑錯）20 道試題，則全數刪除。

三、Part 7 **閱讀**：分成單篇閱讀和雙篇閱讀兩種。

　　單篇閱讀有8~10篇文章，每一篇考2~4題測驗題（第153題~180題）；雙篇閱讀有四組(8篇)文章，每兩篇一組，接著有五道測驗題，共四組8篇20題（第181題~200題）。

　　筆者不惴孤陋、能力淺薄，今針對*New* TOEIC變動較大的Part 6 **短文克漏字**及Part 7 **單篇和雙篇文章閱讀**，各試作一組試題範例介紹於后：

Questions 141-144 refer to the following article.

Practice! Practice! Practice! Although mind-mapping is still a new mnemonic skill, you should feel a great sense of accomplishment in using it frequently.

Probably the best way to learn how to draw a mind map is by studying examples others have drawn. Feel free to copy what you like and ignore everything else. This is flexible and creative too.

Some will use mind-mapping for _____ issues _____

141. (A) solvable	**142.** (A) for
(B) common	(B) while
(C) easy	(C) since
(D) complex	(D) but

others will use it for more simple purposes. The measure of success is in finding, learning, and using mind-mapping that will _____ you to

143. (A) cause
     (B) induce
     (C) lead
     (D) carry

new ways of thinking. I measure my personal success by the degree to which this tool helps you. I hope the use of mind-mapping will make your life and work more organized, imaginative, creative and _____ !

144. (A) effectible
     (B) efficient
     (C) effective
     (D) effectual

　　練習！練習！練習！雖然繪心智圖還是一種新的記憶技巧，但是經常用它，應該會讓你有很大的成就感。

　　學習繪心智圖的最好方法，可能就是參考其他人畫好的範例。不管其他，盡量模仿自己喜歡的。這也是有彈性的和有創意的。

　　有些人會用心智圖在複雜的議題上，而有些人則運用在更簡單的目的。成功的評量標準，就是找到、學習和使用繪心智圖，引領自己到新的思考模式。我衡量我個人的成果，是心智圖對你的幫助有多大而定。我希望，運用繪心智圖，可以讓你的生活和工作更有條理、更有想像力、更有創意和更有效率！

解　答

141 (D) complex　　　　**142** (B) while

143 (C) lead　　　　　**144** (B) efficient

單　字

· mind-mapping	*n.* 繪心智圖	· mnemonic	*a.* 記憶的
· accomplishment	*n.* 成就，實現	· ignore	*v.* 忽視，忽略
· flexible	*a.* 有彈性的	· issue	*n.* 議題，問題
· solvable	*a.* 可解決的	· complex	*a.* 複雜的
· induce	*v.* 勸誘，誘導	· effectible	*a.* 可實現的，可產生的
· effective	*a.* 有效的	· efficient	*a.* 有效率的
· effectual	*a.* 奏效的，有效的		

◎ **Part 7** 單篇閱讀 範例

Questions 153-154 refer to the following note.

****

      ✔ **Listen at moderate volume to avoid hearing damage.**

      ✔ **Do not wear the headphones while driving or cycling.**

✔ **You should use extreme caution or temporarily discontinue use in potentially hazardous situations, such as walking, jogging, etc.**

✔ **Wear them properly: L is left, R is right.**

✔ **This model is supplied with either in-ear type or headband type headphones. When using the in-ear type, wear them with the longer cord behind your neck.**

****

153. What may wearing the headphones cause while biking?
(A) Hearing damage
(B) Headache
(C) Car accident
(D) Fire disaster

154. What does the passage describe?
(A) An electric appliances advertisement
(B) A walkman note on listening with the earphone
(C) A note on cassette tapes
(D) A precaution against fire

問題 **153-154** 請參考以下的須知

****

✔ 以適度的音量收聽，避免聽力受損。
✔ 開車或騎腳踏車時，勿戴耳機。

✔ 在可能會有危險的情況下，如走路、慢跑等，你應該特別注意，或暫時停止使用耳機。
✔ 正確地配戴耳機：**L** 表左邊，**R** 表右邊。
✔ 本產品提供的型式，屬耳塞型或頭箍式的耳機。使用耳塞型耳機時，把較長的線繞到頸後，才戴上耳機。

****

153

What may wearing the headphones cause while biking?	騎單車戴耳機，會造成什麼問題？	正解 (C)

(A) Hearing damage
(B) Headache
(C) Car accident
(D) Fire disaster

(A) 聽力受損
(B) 頭痛
(C) 交通意外
(D) 火災

154

What does the passage describe?	這篇文章描述什麼？	正解 (B)

(A) An electric appliances advertisement
(B) A walkman note on listening with the earphone
(C) A note on cassette tapes
(D) A precaution against fire

(A) 電器用品的廣告
(B) 使用耳機收聽的隨身聽須知
(C) 錄音機卡帶的說明
(D) 防火措施

Word Bank

· moderate	*a.* 適度的，適量的	· volume	*n.* 音量
· cycling = biking	*n.* 騎腳踏車	· temporarily	*adv.* 暫時地
· discontinue	*v.* 中斷	· potentially	*adv.* 潛在地
· hazardous	*a.* 危險的	· jogging	*n.* 慢跑
· headband	*n.* 束髮帶，頭箍	· disaster	*n.* 災難
· appliance	*n.* 電器用品(設備)	· walkman	*n.* 隨身聽
· precaution	*n.* 預防措施	· headphone = earphone	*n.* 耳機

Questions 181-185 refer to the following flyer and invitation.

Let's dance the tango!

Do you like to dance? Do you like tight clothing? The tango just may be the dance for you!

I have been studying the tango for 5 years in Argentina, and now that I have returned to America, I want to keep dancing it! And I want to teach it to others! Anyone! The local community college has agreed to loan me a large room where we can dance as long as I get 20 or more people together!

I have a large stereo that we can play the tango music on (unless you know a good tango band) and so all we need are the people! If you are interested, please call **Jackie** at **(206) 997-0601**. I can't wait to hear from you!

Tea Party at Sara's House

Saturday afternoon at 1 p.m.

Come one come all to the annual super fancy tea party for all of Sara's acquaintances.

Anyone who knows me or knows someone who knows me is welcome.

All you have to bring is yourself, a tea cup, and if possible a sweet treat that goes well with black tea.

I also plan to have non-caffeinated tea for those who get the jitters.

Also, for those who have the courage, recital readings from my copy of Lewis Carroll's Alice in Wonderland would be greatly appreciated.

R.S.V.P. not required. Just come!

讓我們一起跳探戈！

你喜歡跳舞嗎？你喜歡穿緊身衣嗎？
探戈就是你最好的選擇！

　　我在阿根廷學了五年的探戈，現在回到了美國，很想繼續跳下去！也想教其他人！任何人均可！

　　本地社區大學已經同意借給我一個很大的場地，只要我能找到20個人以上！我有一個超大音響，可以播放探戈舞曲（除非你認識一個很好的探戈樂團），所以我們只需要人來！

　　如果你有興趣，請打**Jackie**的電話**(206)997-0601**。我期待著您的來電。

莎拉家辦茶會

週六下午一點

　　所有認識莎拉的朋友，大家都可以來參加一年一度別緻的茶會。

　　歡迎認識我或認識我朋友的人都來參加。

　　只要你人來就好，外加一個茶杯，如果可以的話，就帶一份適合配紅茶的甜點。

　　我也為那些會心悸的人，準備無咖啡因的茶飲。

　　還有，非常歡迎那些有勇氣的人，你們可以朗誦我的一本Lewis Carroll所寫的愛麗斯夢遊仙境。

　　不需要回函，人來就好！

181

What kind of experience does Jackie have with this dance?

(A) 5 year teaching experience
(B) 5 year show experience
(C) 5 year working experience
(D) 5 year dancing experience

Jackie對這項舞蹈有何經驗？ 正解 **(D)**

(A) 五年教學經驗
(B) 五年演出經驗
(C) 五年工作經驗
(D) 五年跳舞經驗

182

What does Jackie have to do to get the room?

(A) Get 5 people together.
(B) Get 20 people together.
(C) Have a large stereo.
(D) Have a tango band.

為了要使用教室，Jackie必 正解 **(B)** 須做什麼？

(A) 找五個人一起。
(B) 找二十個人一起。
(C) 有個大型音響。
(D) 有個探戈舞團。

183

According to the flyer and invitation, what should those who are interested do?

(A) Go directly to the college.
(B) Wear tight clothing.
(C) Call Jackie or just come to the tea party.
(D) Call the college or Sara.

有興趣的人應該怎麼做？ 正解 **(C)**

(A) 直接到學校。
(B) 穿緊身衣。
(C) 打電話給Jackie或直接參加茶會。
(D) 打電話給學校或Sara。

184

What should one bring to the party?

(A) Tea, a copy of Alice in Wonderland, and oneself.
(B) A tea cup, oneself, and if possible a sweet treat.
(C) A tea cup, a book, and the R.S.V.P.
(D) A friend, and someone who knows Sara.

應該帶什麼去參加派對？　　正解 (B)

(A) 茶、一本愛麗斯夢遊仙境和本人。
(B) 一個茶杯、本人，如果可以的話，一樣甜點。
(C) 一個茶杯、一本書和回函。
(D) 一個朋友和認識莎拉的人。

185

What kinds of tea will be served?

(A) Herb tea and non-caffeinated.
(B) Non-caffeinated herb tea.
(C) Caffeinated herb tea.
(D) Black and non-caffeinated.

會供應何種茶？　　正解 (D)

(A) 花草茶和無咖啡因的茶。
(B) 無咖啡因的花草茶。
(C) 含咖啡因的花草茶。
(D) 紅茶和無咖啡因的茶。

Word Bank

· flyer	*n.* 傳單	· tango	*n.* 探戈舞（曲）
· tight clothing	緊身衣	· Argentina	*n.* 阿根廷
· community college	社區大學	· loan	*v.* 借貸
· stereo	*n.* 立體音響	· can't wait to ~	迫不及待
· hear from ~	收到來信或來電	· annual	*a.* 每年的，全年的
· fancy	*a.* 特製的，特選的	· acquaintance	*n.* 認識（之人）
· sweet treat	甜食	· go well with ~	與～搭配良好
· non-caffeinated	*a.* 不含咖啡因的	· jitters	*n.* 心神不定
· recital	*n.* 朗誦	· Alice in Wonderland	(書名)愛麗絲夢遊仙境
· R.S.V.P. (原為法文，請束用語)請賜覆		· herb	*n.* 藥草，香草
· serve	*v.* 供應，供給	· caffeine	*n.* 咖啡因

CD 2　No. 1~8

New TOEIC
Practice Test
中文翻譯和解答

LISTENING TEST

In the Listening test, you will be asked to demonstrate how well you understand spoken English. The entire Listening test will last approximately 45 minutes. There are four parts, and directions are given for each part. You must mark your answers on the separate answer sheet. Do not write your answers in the test book.

Part 1

Directions: For each question in this part, you will hear four statements about a picture in your test book. When you hear the statements, you must select the one statement that best describes what you see in the picture. Then find the number of the question on your answer sheet and mark your answer. The statements will not be printed in your test book and will be spoken only one time.

Sample Answer

Ⓐ Ⓑ **Ⓒ** Ⓓ

Statement (C), "They're standing near the table," is the best description of the picture, so you should select answer (C) and mark it on your answer sheet.

1.

2.

GO ON TO THE NEXT PAGE.

3.

4.

5.

6.

GO ON TO THE NEXT PAGE.

新｜版｜多｜益｜測｜驗｜解｜析

7.

8.

9.

10.

GO ON TO THE NEXT PAGE.

新|版|多|益|測|驗|解|析

Part 2

Directions: You will hear a question or statement and three responses spoken in English. They will be spoken only one time and will not be printed in your test book. Select the best response to the question or statement and mark the letter (A), (B), or (C) on your answer sheet. For example,

You will hear :　　Where is the meeting room?
You will also hear :　(A) To meet the new director.
　　　　　　　　　　(B) It's the first room on the right.
　　　　　　　　　　(C) Yes, at two o'clock.

Sample Answer

The best response to the question "Where is the meeting room?" is choice (B), "It's the first room on the right," so (B) is the correct answer. You should mark answer (B) on your answer sheet.

11. Mark your answer on your answer sheet.
12. Mark your answer on your answer sheet.
13. Mark your answer on your answer sheet.
14. Mark your answer on your answer sheet.
15. Mark your answer on your answer sheet.
16. Mark your answer on your answer sheet.
17. Mark your answer on your answer sheet.
18. Mark your answer on your answer sheet.
19. Mark your answer on your answer sheet.
20. Mark your answer on your answer sheet.
21. Mark your answer on your answer sheet.
22. Mark your answer on your answer sheet.
23. Mark your answer on your answer sheet.
24. Mark your answer on your answer sheet.
25. Mark your answer on your answer sheet.

26. Mark your answer on your answer sheet.
27. Mark your answer on your answer sheet.
28. Mark your answer on your answer sheet.
29. Mark your answer on your answer sheet.
30. Mark your answer on your answer sheet.
31. Mark your answer on your answer sheet.
32. Mark your answer on your answer sheet.
33. Mark your answer on your answer sheet.
34. Mark your answer on your answer sheet.
35. Mark your answer on your answer sheet.
36. Mark your answer on your answer sheet.
37. Mark your answer on your answer sheet.
38. Mark your answer on your answer sheet.
39. Mark your answer on your answer sheet.
40. Mark your answer on your answer sheet.

Part 3

Directions: You will hear some conversations between two people. You will be asked to answer three questions about what the speakers say in each conversation. Select the best response to each question and mark the letter (A), (B), (C), or (D) on your answer sheet. The conversations will be spoken only one time and will not be printed in your test book.

41. What did they decide to do?
- (A) Postpone the picnic
- (B) Cancel the picnic
- (C) Have a picnic
- (D) Plan a picnic

42. According to the conversation, how was the weather earlier this morning?
- (A) It was pouring.
- (B) It was drizzling.
- (C) It was showering.
- (D) It was raining hard.

43. When should the man notify everyone of the change?
- (A) In the evening
- (B) At night
- (C) Until tomorrow
- (D) In the morning

44. What did the man expect to do?
- (A) To do television commercials.
- (B) To work on an advertising project.
- (C) To get into business management.
- (D) To get a temporary job.

45. What did the man do?
- (A) He worked as a doctor.
- (B) He worked in advertising.
- (C) He was a marketing manager.
- (D) He was a businessman.

46. What is the woman working on?
- (A) A customers' survey
- (B) A beauty contest
- (C) A training program
- (D) An interview with a candidate

GO ON TO THE NEXT PAGE.

新 | 版 | 多 | 益 | 測 | 驗 | 解 | 析

47. When will Smith be back?
(A) Within the week
(B) In a week
(C) After two weeks
(D) Today

48. Where is the error?
(A) In the figures
(B) At the end of the report
(C) In the middle of the report
(D) In the beginning of the report

49. Who is the woman?
(A) Smith's secretary
(B) The man's mother
(C) The man's coworker
(D) An usher

_____

50. What does the man want to do?
(A) Check the magazine for an advertisement.
(B) Order a magazine subscription.
(C) Have copies of a magazine made.
(D) Place an advertisement in a magazine.

51. What does the man want to order?
(A) An earlier copy of Inside Business
(B) A back issue of Business World
(C) A current issue of Business World
(D) A current copy of Inside

52. How will the woman get the information for the man?
(A) By going online
(B) By contacting the publisher
(C) By ordering a magazine
(D) By advertising in a magazine

_____

53. Why is the merger proposal unacceptable?
(A) It does not reflect the company's true value.
(B) It is Intertech's first offer.
(C) Intertech Incorporated may not give much more.
(D) The company's stock is too expensive.

54. Why isn't the speakers' company going to get the contract?
(A) Intertech didn't get any good offers.
(B) They were not ready to sign in time.
(C) Intertech got a better deal somewhere else.
(D) Both companies didn't come to an agreement.

55. How did the man feel about the merger?
(A) It is unalterable.
(B) It is highly profitable.
(C) It is unjust.
(D) It is unlawful.

56. What does the woman want to do first?
   (A) Take lunch
   (B) Prepare the evening's meeting
   (C) Ask the man for his opinion
   (D) Revise her sales report

57. What kind of questions does the man _____ have?
   (A) Personal
   (B) Unrelated
   (C) In-depth
   (D) Brief

58. At what stage is the preparation of the promotion meeting?
   (A) Finished
   (B) Well prepared
   (C) Preliminary
   (D) Final

_____

59. How many votes are needed to support the man's proposal?
   (A) 8 votes
   (B) At least one more
   (C) At least 10
   (D) All 15 votes

60. Who is the man?
   (A) A supporter of the proposal
   (B) The chairman of the Board
   (C) The company's founder
   (D) The author of the proposal

61. Who is the woman?
   (A) The man's colleague
   (B) A director of the company
   (C) The general president of the company
   (D) A cleaner

62. Why does the man want to make an appointment?
   (A) He wants to have a medical checkup.
   (B) He wants to see a dentist.
   (C) He wants to visit the pharmacy.
   (D) He wants a new schedule.

63. What could the woman's occupation be?
   (A) A waitress
   (B) A doctor
   (C) A sales check
   (D) A receptionist

64. What will the man do first when he needs a checkup?
   (A) Go to the pharmaceutical department.
   (B) Go on a date with the woman.
   (C) Buy cold medicine.
   (D) Check his schedule and set a date.

_____

GO ON TO THE NEXT PAGE.

新 | 版 | 多 | 益 | 測 | 驗 | 解 | 析

65. What was damaged the most?
    (A) The car
    (B) The woman
    (C) The car driver
    (D) The auto mechanic

66. How does the woman seem?
    (A) depressed
    (B) disappointed
    (C) excited
    (D) emotionally tense

67. What does the man suggest the woman do?
    (A) Start a new job
    (B) Rest for a few days
    (C) Repair her car
    (D) Forget about the car accident

68. What does the man want from the woman?
    (A) To get married
    (B) To do him a favor
    (C) To tell him of her decision
    (D) To tell her company to make a decision

69. Why didn't the man get a response from the woman?
    (A) His computer was broken.
    (B) He doesn't use e-mail.
    (C) The woman didn't send the e-mail.
    (D) He didn't offer the proposal.

70. How about the proposal?
    (A) It has no problem.
    (B) It'll be revised.
    (C) No one will agree on it.
    (D) The woman will negate it.

Part 4

Directions: You will hear some short talks given by a single speaker. You will be asked to answer three questions about what the speaker says in each short talk. Select the best response to each question and mark the letter (A), (B), (C), or (D) on your answer sheet. The talks will be spoken only one time and will not be printed in your test book.

71. When should passengers with cars return to their cars?
    (A) 10 minutes before landing
    (B) 10 minutes ahead of schedule
    (C) Immediately after the announcement
    (D) After instructed to do so by ferry personnel

72. Who will be allowed to leave before cars?
    (A) People on bicycles
    (B) People who are not on the passenger deck
    (C) People with luggage
    (D) People with small children

73. Who will leave the boat on the left side of the main passenger deck?
    (A) People with bicycles
    (B) People on foot
    (C) People with large packages
    (D) Ferry personnel

74. Why is this person giving a speech?
    (A) The person is retiring
    (B) The person got a promotion
    (C) The person has been awarded a prize
    (D) The person is introducing someone very famous

75. Who is giving this speech?
    (A) A librarian
    (B) A company president
    (C) A researcher
    (D) A novelist

76. What does the speaker specialize in?
    (A) Numerology
    (B) Statistics
    (C) Strategy
    (D) Evolution

77. What is Edward Richardson the head of?
    (A) A banking group
    (B) A steel company
    (C) A unniversity of economics department
    (D) A medium-sized company

78. What was Edward Richardson given an award for?
    (A) His explanations of his company.
    (B) His excitement about politics.
    (C) His appearance on the show **Finance in Review**.
    (D) His ideas on the effects of globalization.

79. What will the award-winner be talking about on the show?
    (A) Finance in Review
    (B) economics
    (C) recent economic changes
    (D) globalization

---

80. Who is being addressed?
    (A) A ship captain
    (B) Airport personnel
    (C) Train passengers
    (D) Cabin crew

81. How long will the current situation continue?
    (A) It is unknown.
    (B) For a short time.
    (C) For hours.
    (D) Until the storm stops.

82. What must the listeners do?
    (A) Sit down
    (B) Fasten people in
    (C) Stop serving meals
    (D) Assist the speaker

---

83. What happened in the south Puget Sound region?
    (A) An anti-government demonstration
    (B) Flooding
    (C) A windstorm
    (D) A store robbery

84. What time of the day did the problem begin?
    (A) Early evening
    (B) Early morning
    (C) Midday
    (D) Midnight

85. What event was interrupted?
    (A) The business of small
        transportations.
    (B) The electric company's daily
        work.
    (C) People's use of water.
    (D) The election.

86. What do passengers have to do to
    get a free flight ?
    (A) Flight a lot and collect more
        miles.
    (B) Go to the ticket counter within
        10 minutes.
    (C) Give up their seat on Flight 177.
    (D) Choose an Asian destination.

87. What has been changed?
    (A) The flight number
    (B) The flight time
    (C) The departure gate
    (D) The ticket prices

88. When will boarding start?
    (A) In 20 minutes
    (B) In 30 minutes
    (C) At 7:20 p.m.
    (D) At 7:50 p.m.

89. Why is this company throwing a
    party?
    (A) The manager of the company is
        retiring.
    (B) The company's revenues
        increased by 15 percent.
    (C) To thank the accounting
        department for the quarterly
        report.
    (D) To show appreciation for an
        increase in company profits.

90. Who may attend the party?
    (A) Employees and clients
    (B) Employees and their families
    (C) Employees only
    (D) Employees and celebrities

91. How many times is the report
    released every year?
    (A) Once a year
    (B) Once half a year
    (C) Two times a quarter
    (D) Four times a year

92. Where is this talk taking place?
    (A) At a camp
    (B) At a hospital
    (C) At a health club
    (D) At a school

93. What must be signed?
    (A) A sales contract
    (B) A sign-in sheet
    (C) A health form
    (D) A file

94. What will be the last activity?
    (A) A tour of the weight room
    (B) Questions will be answered
    (C) A medical checkup
    (D) An outdoor party

95. Where are hors d'oeuvres served?
    (A) In the patio
    (B) In the lobby
    (C) In the atrium
    (D) In your room

96. What service requires a fee?
    (A) Breakfast
    (B) Tea and coffee
    (C) Transportation to tour sites
    (D) Drinks

97. What time does the breakfast end?
    (A) 10:00 a.m.
    (B) 11:00 a.m.
    (C) 4:00 p.m.
    (D) It's available all day.

98. What is being discussed?
    (A) Opening a bank account
    (B) Applying for a credit card
    (C) Sending money
    (D) Finding a good bank

99. What is needed for this process?
    (A) A deposit
    (B) A big bank account
    (C) A signature
    (D) An e-mail address

100. What is an advantage of this?
    (A) You can do it by phone.
    (B) You can get a gift.
    (C) You can go overseas.
    (D) You don't have to sign anything.

■ Stop! This is the end of the listening test.
Turn to Part 5 in your test book.

READING TEST

In the Reading test, you will read a variety of texts and answer several different types of reading comprehension questions. The entire Reading test will last 75 minutes. There are three parts, and directions are given for each part. You are encouraged to answer as many questions as possible within the time allowed.

You must mark your answers on the separate answer sheet. Do not write your answers in the test book.

Part 5
Directions: A word or phrase is missing in each of the sentences below. Four answer choices are given below each sentence. Select the best answer to complete the sentence. Then mark the letter (A), (B), (C), or (D) on your answer sheet.

101. Ms. Max is going to take a trip to Paris with her fiance ------- her holiday.
(A) on
(B) during
(C) in
(D) while

102. They say Mr. Rose has ------- to do with the bankruptcy of Signtech because he was in another company when it happened.
(A) everything
(B) anything
(C) nothing
(D) something

103. The latest upgraded model ------- the value of Songtech Company, so the company expects to increase its profit.
(A) deflects
(B) causes
(C) accredits
(D) enhances

104. As Carol made repeated mistakes on her night-duty, she was ------- yesterday.
(A) negotiated
(B) duplicated
(C) separated
(D) terminated

GO ON TO THE NEXT PAGE.

新 | 版 | 多 | 益 | 測 | 驗 | 解 | 析

105. The customer service center has received a lot more complaints than expected as ------- May 15.
(A) of
(B) by
(C) since
(D) on

106. The movie theater was ------- with audience on the evening of the fatal fire disaster.
(A) crowd
(B) crowded
(C) crowding
(D) crowds

107. It's best to optimize your press ------- so they can be readily searched and browsed.
(A) news
(B) messages
(C) releases
(D) coverage

108. After going on a hike, Warren realized that he couldn't walk as fast as a few years ago when he was in -------.
(A) cosy
(B) good
(C) perfect
(D) shape

109. Relatively few people ever stop and decide what their top ------- is and work on that first.
(A) priority
(B) priorize
(C) prior
(D) priorties

110. If one wants to ------- a good impression at a job interview, it is best not to smoke or chatter.
(A) have
(B) make
(C) keep
(D) get

111. Our company ------- all employees to wear identification badges when we enter our plant.
(A) slects
(B) requires
(C) admits
(D) concedes

112. The express train ------- at the terminal half hour ago.
(A) arrived
(B) has arrived
(C) had arrived
(D) is arrived

113. The whole workforce felt justified to take strike action because they complained ------- about working conditions.
(A) unlikey
(B) bitterly
(C) carelessly
(D) terribly

114. Professor Wu, ------- born in Taiwan, lived and practiced law in Hong Kong.
(A) even
(B) he was
(C) although
(D) who he was

115. She asked me whether Smith had the capability -------.
(A) doing that
(B) to do that
(C) do that
(D) of doing that

116. In spite of his proposal, the president agreed to consider ------- a raise in salary.
(A) to request
(B) request
(C) requesting
(D) requested

117. All exhibitors ------- their displays since last Friday for the upcoming international trade exhibition.
(A) have prepared
(B) will prepare
(C) prepare
(D) prepared

118. Ms. Thompson is ------- with her money because she wants to buy a gorgeous car.
(A) economic
(B) economical
(C) economized
(D) economically

119. Mr. Douglas always ------- assured that we will be successful on any project he assigns us.
(A) rests
(B) makes
(C) sees
(D) has

120. More than half of the executives firmly believed the president in his financial ------- plan.
(A) resrore
(B) restoration
(C) restored
(D) restorative

GO ON TO THE NEXT PAGE.

121. The smart marketers of today create compelling messages and tell prospective customers directly ------- Web-powered communication tools.
(A) use
(B) uses
(C) using
(D) used

122. We still wonder who will make a business ------- to Singapore to negotiate with Northwest Technology.
(A) travel
(B) tour
(C) trip
(D) journey

123. Lifetech company is privately held and does not disclose -------, but it is clear this is a growing business.
(A) perks
(B) savings
(C) income
(D) revenues

124. Before being traded to the Panthers, he ------- the greatest relief pitcher in the long history of the Eagles.
(A) had been
(B) is
(C) has been
(D) will be

125. Wanda and Harvey ------- to Hawaii next fall even though it is a very busy time for them.
(A) are coming
(B) aren't coming
(C) have come
(D) came

126. You should not criticize someone until you --------in his shoes.
(A) talk a while
(B) walk a mile
(C) work all day
(D) work a while

127. He thought the sales meeting was on Thursday or Friday so imagine his surprise when he found out it was going to ------- on Saturday.
(A) be held
(B) have held
(C) hold
(D) hold on

128. They are on the company's expense account and can run ------- the bill as high as they like.
(A) down
(B) out
(C) over
(D) up

129. Las Vegas has many conventions and is very crowded at that time of year so you should ------- a hotel room well in advance of your visit.
(A) book
(B) call
(C) make
(D) reservation

130. The sales department has spent over a month working on this proposal so if they get turned ------- they will be very disappointed.
(A) down
(B) in
(C) over
(D) up

131. It is a long application but you only have to ------- in the boxes that are marked to save you some time.
(A) call
(B) sign
(C) drop
(D) fill

132. Because she was such a generous and caring person, many people ------- kindly of her at her retirement party.
(A) gave
(B) said
(C) spoke
(D) took

133. Right now we are doing well because we were able to anticipate the downturn in the economy while the other companies ------- like the boom would last forever.
(A) acted
(B) have acted
(C) will acted
(D) act

134. With the low morale of the office and the sad state of the economy, there is -------we would ever take on another project right now.
(A) another way
(B) a way
(C) no way
(D) some way

135. This meeting may have to take longer than we expected if we are going to ------- at an agreement we can all live with.
(A) arrive
(B) get
(C) laugh
(D) look

GO ON TO THE NEXT PAGE.

新 | 版 | 多 | 益 | 測 | 驗 | 解 | 析

136. The forest fires burned for three days until the soldiers and firefighters were able to get the situation ------- .
(A) prohibited
(B) out of control
(C) safe
(D) under control

137. According to the news, there were ------- 100 people trapped in the building at the time of the fire.
(A) estimated
(B) an estimated
(C) the estimating
(D) estimation

138. Raymond could barely ------- his smile at the thought of how much money he was going to make.
(A) contain
(B) envelop
(C) maintain
(D) include

139. The customer's visits to the plant are too ------- for the manager to get acquainted with her.
(A) unfamiliar
(B) efficient
(C) definite
(D) infrequent

140. Every month we keep getting more and more instructions, and they are getting too hard to keep ------- with.
(A) ahead
(B) down
(C) forward
(D) up

Part 6

Directions: Read the texts below. A word or phrase is missing in some of the sentences. For each empty space in the text, select the best answer to complete the text. Then mark the letter (A), (B), (C), or (D) on your answer sheet.

Questions 141-143 refer to the following message.

Which is more valuable? To provide a $60,000 heart transplant for an _____ child of indigent parents? Or to use that money

141. (A) ail
 (B) ailed
 (C) ailing
 (D) ailment

for prenatal care that may enhance the life expectancy of fetuses being carried by 100 expectant mothers? Surely the leaders of the democratic capitalist world can afford both. _____ a growing

142. (A) Although
 (B) Yet
 (C) When
 (D) Then

number of health experts argue that most developed countries, in fact, no longer has the financial resources to provide _____

143. (A) unlimited
 (B) infinite
 (C) exclusive
 (D) profitable

medical treatment for all those who need it. The only solution, they say, is rationing health care.

GO ON TO THE NEXT PAGE.

Everybody wants to look healthy and feel energetic. Getting in shape requires exercise. Some people make their decisions to get back into shape with a _____ to the mall to buy

144. (A) trip
(B) travel
(C) sightseeing
(D) glance

exercise outfits and equipment that can cost hundreds of dollars while others spend a lot of money on fitness center memberships. What a senseless waste it is!

_____ , if you do make the decision to start

145. (A) Supposedly
(B) Therefore
(C) Likewise
(D) Otherwise

exercising, start slowly. If you jog, you can find a good pair of running shoes for 60-70 dollars. If you join a health club, try a _____ membership. Before you make that big purchase

146. (A) tried
(B) try
(C) trial
(D) trying

for fitness, make sure you have the willpower to get in shape first.

Having been made possible by improvements in international shipping, now it is easier to send computer parts and raw materials nearly anywhere today _____ a much less expensive

147. (A) at
   (B) in
   (C) on
   (D) with

price than 20 years ago. However, one change of the technology has meant a steep rise in production costs for every computermaker. Consumers are demanding a higher rate of perfection today. At present, a problem with production can also mean a class action, but years ago it would only have necessitated a _____.

148. (A) withdrawal
   (B) protection
   (C) recall
   (D) termination

Therefore new and expensive technologies have _____ to

149. (A) come
   (B) gone
   (C) turned
   (D) gotten

be used to minimize the possibility of making defective computers.

GO ON TO THE NEXT PAGE.

Questions 150-152 refer to the following letter.

Dear Friend,

    The Anti-Pollution Committee of the Super Sugar Refinery is pleased to inform you that an anti-pollution program will be started for nearby residents next month.

    It is our aim to win the residents' support of this district to fight pollution. Due to the fact that you have recently moved _____ the newly-completed estate of Grand Building, it is

150. (A) around
      (B) on
      (C) into
      (D) up

with much pleasure that our Committee is going to provide service to you as well.

    To publicize the work of our Committee, an anti-pollution program _____ especially for the residents of Grand

151. (A) erupted
      (B) held
      (C) ended
      (D) concluded

Building includes a press conference and door-to-door visits. The press conference will be held on Saturday morning (May 25). As for the visits which will mainly be _____ in the

152. (A) selected
      (B) engaged
      (C) erected
      (D) conducted

evening between 8 p.m. and 10 p.m. from Monday thru Thursday, our Committee would appreciate an opportunity to meet with you to explain our services in detail.

    If there are any questions, please call our free number, 0800-123-123.

Yours faithfully,

Smith Wang

Smith Wang
Chairman,
Anti-Pollution Committee of Super Sugar Refinery

Part 7

Directions: In this part you will read a selection of texts, such as magazine and newspaper articles, letters, and advertisements. Each text is followed by several questions. Select the best answer for each question and mark the letter (A), (B), (C), or (D) on your answer sheet.

Questions 153-154 refer to the following letter.

HSC Motors Company, Inc.
1234 Juarez Ave.,
Hermosa, CA 87342

Dear New Car Owner,

    Thank you for your recent purchase of a 2008 HSC sports utility vehicle.
    Customer safety and satisfaction is the number one concern for us here at HSC Motors. Therefore, we are contacting all owners of the 2008 CoSpeed TEC to alert them to a potential malfunction in the brake light electrical system of this model. It has come to our attention that in some instances, the brake lights fail to turn off when the brake pedal is no longer depressed.
    Our electrical engineers have developed a simple and easy-to-install device for this problem. It would be our pleasure to have this installed for you at no cost. In order to make this as convenient as possible for you, your nearest HSC Motors dealers will dispatch a mechanic to your home or work, at no extra charge. Installations may also be done at your dealership. Simply call the dealership where your CoSpeed was purchased to set up an appointment. We truly apologize for any inconvenience.

Sincerely,

Juan Howard

Executive Vice-President,
Sales Development

---

153. What is the purpose of this letter?

(A) To inform engineers of a design flaw.
(B) To advertise a new car model.
(C) To recommend tips on driver safety.
(D) To announce a parts replacement.

154. Why would customers call their dealership?

(A) To get someone to come over and fix the problem.
(B) To complain about the services.
(C) To talk to an engineer about the brake pedal.
(D) To purchase a new CoSpeed at a discount.

A University of Denger poll of young people found some intriguing opinions about adulthood and maturity. Considering most kids start college at age 17 or 18, it's almost comical that the average age most expected to find a full-time job is 21.2. This either means a lot of kids take about three long years to find a full-time job after high school graduation or that college kids are skipping graduation ceremonies altogether and getting almost a year's head start in the job market. The poll did not break down the respondents according to education levels and has therefore left its findings open to a lot of criticism. Even so, the full results are fascinating:

Goal in life	Average age expected to achieve this goal
Self-support	20.9 years old
Moving out from parents' home	21.1 years old
First full-time job	21.2 years old
College graduation	22.3 years old
Financially able to support a family	24.5 years old
Married	25.7 years old
Birth of first child	26.2 years old

155. When do those polled think they should leave home?

(A) At 20.9 years of age.
(B) At 21.1 years of age.
(C) At 21.2 years of age.
(D) At 22.3 years of age.

156. Why do some people criticize the results?

(A) The education level of the respondents is not given.
(B) The number of the respondents is too small.
(C) The questions are comical.
(D) Older people were not polled.

157. How soon after college do the young people polled expect to be married?

(A) About 2 years.
(B) Within 3 years.
(C) About 3 and a half years.
(D) Four and a half years after.

※ *One-Hour Tours*

Across the waterfront. Departs at 12:00, 1:00, 2:00 and 3:00 from Point Hudson's Long Dock. Saturdays and Sundays only by this schedule. By charter weekdays. **$6**

※ *Two-Hour Tours*

Expanded waterfront tour, to view the waterfront, the Fort and Point Wilson areas. Depart and return at the Boat Haven Dock. Departs 12:30 weekdays only. **$12**

※ *Three-Hour Tours*

Leisurely ride to Sims Harbor, landing at Nordland's General Store as tides allow. By advanced reservation only. Departs 8:30 a.m. DAILY from Boat Haven Dock. **$20**

158. What is true about the information?
(A) The one-hour tours depart from Boat Haven Dock.
(B) The two-hour tours are scheduled only on weekdays.
(C) A three-hour tour costs twelve dollars.
(D) The leisurely rides land at Nordland's General Store daily.

159. Which tour requires reservations?
(A) The two-hour tours.
(B) The three-hour tours.
(C) The expanded waterfront tours.
(D) They all require reservations.

Questions 160-162 refer to the following information.

- Orlando pledges 1% of sales to the preservation and restoration of the natural environment. For further information, please write to Orlando Environmental Program, Box 1019, Ventura, CA 94126.
- For a catalog, the name of your nearest dealer, or further information, call 1-800-530-9224 (U.S.A. and Canada only) or check out our Web site: www.orlando.com
- Please contact the store from which you bought your Orlando product for a refund, exchange or repair. For certain items, damage due to wear and tear will be repaired at a reasonable charge.

Care: Machine wash in cold water, gentle cycle. Line dry. Do not bleach.

160. What is NOT included in this information?
(A) How to wash the item.
(B) How to contact the company.
(C) How to get a catalog.
(D) How to reach the company by e-mail.

161. What happens to 1% of the company's sales?
(A) It is given as bonuses to the management.
(B) It goes to the renovation of stores.
(C) It goes to charity.
(D) It is returned to the customers.

162. What best describes this company?
(A) Energy-efficient.
(B) Environmentally conscious.
(C) Cost-cutting.
(D) Anti-globalization.

Dear Ms. Hartford,

If you watched the nightly news, by now you have heard the news of last night's fire that all but destroyed the Midwest Savings and Loan Association. As a depositor, no doubt this has raised your concern. But I am writing you as president of the institution to assure you that your savings is safe and we are well on the way to recovery.

It is true that the fire has completely destroyed our physical location. You will no longer be able to transact business at our Meadowland Road headquarters. But technology has enabled us to save the bulk of our operation, and your files and records are safe in our offsite storage facility. We will be ready to transact business within two days of your receiving this letter.

A temporary facility has been established at 2900 Broomsfield Court, where we will process over-the-counter transactions. If you have a checking account with us, your checks will continue to be accepted and processed through Greydon Trust, our correspondent bank. Your savings, insured by the Federal Deposit Insurance Corp., are available to you any time.

If you have any specific questions, feel free to call the Midwest hotline at 800-999-1234. We thank you for your patience. A disaster like this is never easy to overcome, but your support makes it that much easier.

Best regards,

Robert Hendricks

Robert Hendricks
President, Midwest Savings and Loan Association

GO ON TO THE NEXT PAGE.

163. Why was this letter sent?
    (A) To let depositors know that fires
        at the bank are very unusual.
    (B) To warn depositors of a fire at
        the bank.
    (C) To ask depositors for help in
        rebuilding the bank.
    (D) To assure depositors at the
        bank that their money is safe.

164. What can depositors do until a
    permanent bank is established?
    (A) Use the temporary bank.
    (B) Wait a few days until the new
        bank is built.
    (C) Open a checking account at
        Greydon Trust.
    (D) Call the Federal Deposit
        Insurance Corp. to withdraw
        money.

165. How about the depositors' files
    and records ?
    (A) They were in a safe box in the
        basement.
    (B) They were stored in another
        place.
    (C) The money is safe.
    (D) The bank is asking for
        depositors to support bank
        anyway.

166. Why is the depositor's money
    available?
    (A) It is insured.
    (B) It was in a separate vault.
    (C) Donations will cover most of it.
    (D) With depositor's support the
        bank will not suffer.

Dear Sir or Madam,

First of all, we at Via San Remo would like to extend our deepest gratitude for your continued patronage throughout the years. We find that, in these difficult economic times, the cost of maintaining the restaurant at the level at which we have served the community far exceeds projected revenue in the future. Thus, with deep regret, we are closing our doors after 25 years of business in the area.

We will be open for business, with regular business hours, until June 30th. Again, we'd like to thank you and we hope to see you once again. You have been a valued customer and we will surely miss you, your family and guests.

Sincerely,
the Management

167. What is the purpose of this letter?
(A) To announce a grand opening.
(B) To introduce new management staff.
(C) To inform of a closing.
(D) To notify customers of new business hours.

168. What is this business' current situation?
(A) It is located in a bad area.
(B) It is re-opening elsewhere.
(C) It is undergoing financial difficulties.
(D) Its management has quit.

169. What kind of person will receive this letter?
(A) A regular customer.
(B) A picky customer.
(C) Someone who comes in for the first time.
(D) Someone who gets acquainted with the manager.

170. Who is this letter from?
(A) The owner.
(B) The host and hostess.
(C) The managing staff.
(D) The head chef.

GO ON TO THE NEXT PAGE.

Tahini (Sesame Paste) Salad Dressing

- 2 cloves fresh garlic, crushed
- Half-cup sesame paste
- Quarter-cup soy sauce
- Quarter-cup lemon juice
- Half cup virgin olive oil
- Quarter-cup water
- 1 teaspoon ground cayenne pepper
- 1 teaspoon black pepper

In a saucepan, sauté the fresh, crushed garlic in the olive oil. Do this as slowly as possible and at the lowest flame so that the garlic flavor comes out into the oil as much as possible and because virgin olive oil has a very delicate flavor that can be ruined by too much heat.

Combine the sesame paste and water in a mixing bowl and mix with a wire whisk until creamy smooth with no lumps. Doing this before adding other ingredients makes the sesame paste easier to handle. Add the soy sauce and lemon juice and cayenne and black pepper. When the garlic has sautéed for as long as possible, but before turning brown, add the garlic and olive oil, and whisk until evenly mixed. Drizzle on your favorite salads, or even on fresh, steaming bread.

171. Why should the sauté heat be low?
- (A) So that you can follow the other directions at the same time.
- (B) So you don't burn the pan.
- (C) To keep the flavor of the garlic and olive oil best.
- (D) To conserve resources.

172. How long should you mix the sesame paste?
- (A) Until it is bubbly.
- (B) For 5 to 7 minutes.
- (C) As long as is needed.
- (D) Until it has no lumps.

173. Why should you mix the sesame paste and water before other ingredients?
- (A) The other ingredients will ruin the flavor.
- (B) The sesame paste will become easier to work with.
- (C) The sesame paste will become richer.
- (D) The other ingredients get in the way.

174. Fllowing the recipe's instructions, what can one make ?
- (A) sesame paste
- (B) salad dressing
- (C) pepper sauce
- (D) sautéed garlic

Questions 175-176 refer to the following memo.

M E M O

DATE: October 11, 2008
TO: All Employees
FROM: Carol Katster, Operations Manager

This is to notify you that as of Monday, Octorber 18, our telephone system will be fully automated. We will no longer have operators nor a main switchboard. The Human Resources Department will field misdirected calls but will not take messages of any sort. You are responsible for the automated greetings of your personal line and the retrieval of any messages. Please refer to the message center manual that was distributed last week. For further information, please contact your department manager.

175. What is scheduled to take place?
(A) The notification of all employees.
(B) The firing of all telephone personnel.
(C) The automation of their phone system.
(D) The distribution of new telephone lines.

176. What will the Human Resources Department do?
(A) Explain the new system.
(B) Leave message for interviewees.
(C) Pick up certain phone calls.
(D) Leave messages for employees.

Q:

I have a pit bull puppy that is 2 months old, and is beginning to get too rowdy and hard-to-handle. I want to train him, but I don't want to hit him, because I am afraid that hitting him might make him mean when he gets older. What should I do?

A: It is true that hitting an animal can sometimes cause it to become ill-tempered. And besides, you love your puppy, right? So why should you hit it? The answer is in alternative methods to correct bad behavior. Being persistent, and using a stern, strong voice is often all that is needed for your puppy to understand just what you mean. Every time your puppy does something you don't like, respond with a stern "NO!" and gently stop your puppy from jumping up on you or biting. You may be surprised at how puppies will learn to read your feelings just by the sound of your voice if you repeat it the exact same way every time. Remember, the key is repetition and persistence!

177. Why does this person need advice about his or her puppy?
(A) The puppy is unhappy.
(B) The person doesn't like his or her puppy.
(C) The puppy is mean.
(D) The puppy is rowdy.

178. Why doesn't this person want to hit his or her puppy?
(A) It hurts the hand.
(B) When the puppy grows up it might become mean.
(C) When the puppy grows up it might hit others.
(D) When the puppy is mean, it bites.

179. What is the column's advice?
(A) Repeatedly use a stern voice.
(B) Just hit the puppy, it will be OK.
(C) Hit persistently.
(D) Get rid of the puppy.

180. According to the columm, what may hitting an animal cause it?
(A) To become limped.
(B) To become nervous.
(C) To become irritable.
(D) To become friendly.

GO ON TO THE NEXT PAGE.

USED BOOK SALE

Jeffrey's Used Book Warehouse is having its biggest sale ever. The books have piled up so high that there is almost no room to move around here anymore; so all books are on sale! Especially non-fiction! While all fiction is at least 40 percent off, non-fiction is at least 65 percent off ! Some non-fiction as much as 80 percent off ! Our huge store has so many books that you are sure to find something you like! Buy five books and get one free (priced lower than 12 dollars) ! Sale ends at the end of next week.

Due to the confusion over our former library borrowing policy, Roosevelt County Public Library will be revising its system. While reference books were available for checkout on Fridays before (to be returned the following Monday), starting next week all reference will be for use in the library only. All fiction will be available for a one-month checkout period as opposed to the 5 week checkout before. Nonfiction checkout will remain unchanged. Thank you and keep reading!

181. Why is Jeffrey's bookstore having a sale?
(A) The manager said so.
(B) They have too many books.
(C) They want to get more customers.
(D) They like to have sales.

182. Why has the library's system changed?
(A) The librarians were bored with the old system.
(B) The old system confused people.
(C) The old system angered people.
(D) The librarians wanted change.

183. If you bought five books, which book could you get for free?
(A) A fiction book
(B) A book priced lower than twelve dollars
(C) A non-fiction book
(D) Any one of them

184. How long could reference books be checked out?
(A) for one day
(B) for one week
(C) for two weeks
(D) for the weekend

185. How many weeks will all fiction be available for checkout?
(A) Four week
(B) Five weeks
(C) Two weeks
(D) Three weeks

GO ON TO THE NEXT PAGE.

新 | 版 | 多 | 益 | 測 | 驗 | 解 | 析

To:	Book Club Online [order-info@globalview.com]
From:	borisfrette@iphone.com
Subject:	Replacement & Reimbursement
Date:	Sept. 25, 2008

To whom it may concern,

On September 18th I ordered a copy of Deception Point by Dan Brown and a copy of Four Past Midnight by Stephen King under my order number LW2503.

On opening the package received this afternoon, I found that it contained a copy of Different Seasons and a copy of The Green Mile by the same author, Stephen King. I regret that I can't keep these books as I have bought them already. Therefore I am returning these books by express post for immediate replacement, as I am really looking forward to reading the books I ordered.

By the way, I also hope that you would reimburse $3, the postage, for the returned books. Please check your order records, and send the replacement ASAP.

Faithfully yours,

Boris Frette

To:	borisfrette@iphone.com
From:	Book Club Online [order-info@globalview.com]
Subject:	Re: Replacement & Reimbursement
Date:	Sept. 26, 2008

Dear Mr. Frette,

　We are very sorry to learn from your e-mail yesterday that a mistake in dealing with your order was made. The mistake is entirely our own. I sincerely apologize for our neglect and the inconvenience caused to you. This occurred during this unusually busy season and also the fact that our staff were exhausted.

　Two copies of the correct title have been sent to you today. Surely your account will be credited with the invoiced value of the books and the cost of the return postage.

　Our credit note is enclosed and we apologize again for our mistake. Sincerely yours,

Andrew Clave
Manager, Service Center
Book Club Online

----- Original Message -----
From: borisfrette@iphone.com
To: Book Club Online [order-info@globalview.com]
Sent: Sept. 25, 2008 2:32 PM
Subject: Replacement & Reimbursement

186. What did Boris ask for?
   (A) Paying back partially
   (B) Full repayment
   (C) Placing an order
   (D) Exchanging book

187. Who is the writer of Four Past
   Midnight?
   (A) Boris Frette
   (B) Andrew Clave
   (C) Stephen King
   (D) Dan Brown

188. Which of the books did Mr. Frette
   NOT order?
   (A) Deception Point
   (B) The Green Mile
   (C) Four Past Midnight
   (D) Book Club Online

189. Why was the error made?
   (A) The staff were dog-tired.
   (B) The credit note was not
      enclosed.
   (C) The package was broken.
   (D) The order was cancelled.

190. When are the correct books
   delivered?
   (A) Sept. 25
   (B) Sept. 26
   (C) Sept. 18
   (D) afternoon, Sep. 18

To:	service@daffodilrest.com
From:	doberna@hotonline.net
Subject:	Complaints
Date:	September 7, 2008

To the Manager:

My family and I have been regular customers at your establishment for the last seven years. I have always enjoyed not only the food but also the friendly atmosphere and outstanding service.

On Friday, September 5, I was quite shocked to find that you had completely changed your menu and hired a completely new staff without informing your customers. I was told that your restaurant had not been sold but that management had decided to give the restaurant a "facelift" in order to compete with the trendy new restaurant in town.

First of all, it is hard to believe that you gave no notice whatsoever to your customers about all this. Secondly, and more importantly, I see no reason for such drastic changes. You have a sizable base of loyal, satisfied customers who you will surely lose. The new restaurant in town is good but it is a chain restaurant that lacks the home cooking and the home-like atmosphere that were unique to the Daffodil.

We hope you will reconsider the changes you've made at the Daffodil.

Sincerely,

Donald Berna

GO ON TO THE NEXT PAGE.

To:	doberna@hotonline.net
From:	service@daffodilrest.com
Subject:	Re: Complaints
Date:	September 9, 2008

Dear Mr. Berna,

First and foremost, we deeply appreciate this opportunity to show our heartfelt thanks to you for your concern and continued patronage.

The number of restaurants in this area has greatly increased throughout the past few years. Where there used to be family restaurants serving standard American food for example, is now a restaurant row with Mexican, Indian, Japanese, Filipino and Cuban restaurants, just to name a few. The Daffodil has to compete in a commercial environment so we have transformed it into an American style Italian dinnerhouse.

We regret any inconvenience caused by the change of the Daffodil. You are still a valued customer and we are looking forward to your business.

Sincerely yours,

Darren Carmil
Senior Manager, **The Daffodil**

----- Original Message -----
From: doberna@hotonline.net
To: service@daffodilrest.com
Sent: Sept. 7, 2008 3:02 PM
Subject: Complaints

191. What is the general tone of the first e-mail?
(A) Congratulatory
(B) Malicious
(C) Disappointed
(D) Sympathetic

192. What is NOT the Daffodil known for?
(A) Nice meals.
(B) A chain restaurant.
(C) The home cooking.
(D) The home-like atmosphere.

193. What troubles Mr. Berna most?
(A) The Daffodil did not notify its customers.
(B) The Daffodil decided to change locations.
(C) The Daffodil decided to close.
(D) The Daffodil totally changed.

194. When has the increase in international restaurants occurred?
(A) In the past 7 years
(B) In the past few years
(C) On the weekends
(D) In September

195. What has this area like in the past?
(A) Only Americans lived here.
(B) There used to be a lot of traffic.
(C) There were many fast food restaurants.
(D) There were many family restaurants.

Dear Mr. Waltin,

   This is to formally invite you to the reception of our company's 28th anniversary celebration which I have already mentioned to you by phone last week. The reception will be held in the International Convention Hall of the New Oriental Hotel. The formal invitation will be sent to you by express this afternoon.

   The purpose of this reception is just to invite some of the important people who have supported us over the years so that we can show a small token of our gratitude.

   We do hope that you will be able to spare the time to share this historical moment with us.

Sincerely yours,

Lois Vinster

Lois Vinster
Vice president,
Stastech Ltd Company

Dear Ms. Vinster,

No doubt there will be celebration taking place next month at your corporate headquarters, I would like to join those wishing you heartiest congratulations on your 28 years serving the automotive needs of Singaporean consumers.

As a major supplier to your firm for the past 12 years, we appreciate having had the opportunity to help position you as one of the preeminent manufacturers of automotive parts in the country. It has been a beneficial journey for both our firms, and we are glad to have been part of the excitement.

A toast to you on your 28th anniversary! Here's hoping the next 28 years will be even more successful for all of us.

Best regards,

Derek Waltin

Derek Waltin
Senior Vice President,
Cartech Company

196. Who is the writer of the second letter?
(A) A member of a competing firm
(B) A manufacturer of auto parts
(C) A supplier of a car parts maker
(D) A car manufacturer

197. How long have the two firms been connected?
(A) 28 years
(B) 12 years
(C) 40 years
(D) Not specified

198. What does Ms. Vinster's firm do?
(A) Manufactures automobiles
(B) Buys auto parts from manufacturers
(C) Manufactures parts for automobiles
(D) Supplies parts to an auto parts maker

199. How many times will Mr. Waltin have been informed of the invitation message?
(A) 1 time
(B) 2 times
(C) 3 times
(D) Not specified

200. In Vinster's letter, the word " token " in paragraph 2, line 3 is closest in meaning to
(A) symbol
(B) keepsake
(C) lot
(D) coin

■ Stop! This is the end of the test. If you finish before time is called, you may go back to Part 5, 6, and 7 and check your work.

CD 2   No. 1~8

New TOEIC
Practice Test

New TOEIC Practice Test Answer Key

Item Number	Key	Item Number	Key	Item Number	Key	Item Number	Key
1	C	51	A	101	A	151	B
2	C	52	A	102	C	152	D
3	A	53	A	103	D	153	D
4	C	54	D	104	D	154	A
5	C	55	C	105	A	155	B
6	D	56	B	106	B	156	A
7	A	57	C	107	C	157	C
8	D	58	C	108	D	158	B
9	D	59	C	109	A	159	B
10	D	60	D	110	B	160	D
11	C	61	A	111	B	161	C
12	B	62	A	112	A	162	B
13	C	63	D	113	B	163	D
14	A	64	D	114	C	164	A
15	B	65	A	115	B	165	B
16	B	66	D	116	C	166	A
17	C	67	B	117	A	167	C
18	A	68	C	118	B	168	C
19	A	69	A	119	A	169	A
20	B	70	B	120	B	170	C
21	A	71	C	121	C	171	C
22	C	72	A	122	C	172	D
23	A	73	B	123	D	173	B
24	C	74	C	124	A	174	B
25	B	75	C	125	A	175	C
26	A	76	B	126	B	176	C
27	A	77	A	127	A	177	D
28	A	78	D	128	D	178	B
29	A	79	C	129	A	179	A
30	C	80	D	130	A	180	C
31	A	81	B	131	D	181	B
32	B	82	A	132	C	182	B
33	A	83	C	133	A	183	B
34	C	84	B	134	C	184	D
35	B	85	D	135	A	185	A
36	A	86	C	136	D	186	D
37	C	87	C	137	B	187	C
38	A	88	B	138	A	188	B
39	B	89	D	139	D	189	A
40	A	90	B	140	D	190	B
41	A	91	D	141	C	191	C
42	B	92	C	142	B	192	B
43	D	93	C	143	A	193	D
44	C	94	A	144	A	194	B
45	B	95	C	145	B	195	D
46	D	96	C	146	C	196	C
47	B	97	A	147	A	197	B
48	D	98	C	148	C	198	C
49	C	99	C	149	A	199	C
50	A	100	A	150	C	200	A

Part 1　CD 2　No. 2

中　文　翻　譯　和　解　答

1

(A) The man is examining his briefcase.
(B) The man is standing by the door.
(C) The man is looking at his hand.
(D) The man is looking for a woman.

(A) 男子正在檢查他的手提箱。
(B) 男子站在門旁。
(C) 男子正在看著手。
(D) 男子在找一位女士。

- examine　　*v.* 檢查，考試
- briefcase　　*n.* 手提箱，公事包
- look for　　　尋找

正解　**(C)**

2

(A) People are waiting in line.
(B) All of the people are waiting in pairs.
(C) People are sitting on chairs.
(D) This is a well-known diner in this area.

(A) 人們正排隊等候。
(B) 所有的人分組在等待。
(C) 人們坐在椅子上。
(D) 這是這一帶很有名的餐館。

正解　**(C)**

- in pairs　　　　分組，成雙成對
- sign　　　　*n.* 標示（牌），招牌
- well-known　*a.* 著名的，知名的
- diner　　　　*n.* 小餐館

3

(A) One building is cylindrical.
(B) The building has a helipad on the rooftop.
(C) The square building is the tallest in this city.
(D) These buildings have fallen over

(A) 有一棟建築物是圓柱形的。
(B) 這棟建築物的屋頂上有直昇機機場。
(C) 這棟方型大樓是市區裡最高的建築。
(D) 這些建築物都已倒塌了。

正解 **(A)**

‧ cylindrical	*a.* 圓柱形的		‧ helipad	*n.* 直昇機機場
‧ rooftop	*n.* 屋頂		‧ square	*a.* （正）方形的
‧ fall over	倒塌			

4

(A) The woman is reclining on the counter
(B) The woman is restoring magazines to the shelf
(C) The woman is reaching out with her hand.
(D) The woman is removing an item from a rack.

(A) 女士斜躺在櫃台。
(B) 女士在整理書架上的雜誌。
(C) 女士正伸出她的手。
(D) 女士從架上拿出一件東西。

正解 **(C)**

‧ recline	*v.* 斜靠，斜躺		‧ restore	*v.* 重整，重建
‧ magazine	*n.* 雜誌		‧ shelf	*n.* 架子，層架
‧ reach out	伸出		‧ remove	*v.* 移出，去除
‧ item	*n.* 物品，產品		‧ rack	*n.* 置物架，架子
‧ counter	*n.* 櫃台			

中　文　翻　譯　和　解　答

5

(A) All of the seats are occupied at the moment.
(B) The desks are grouped in a circle.
(C) The wastebaskets are on a plain carpet.
(D) There is no room to walk in this office.

(A) 所有的座位此刻都被佔滿了。
(B) 所有的桌子都圍成一圈。
(C) 垃圾桶放在素面地毯上。
(D) 這辦公室沒有空間可以走動。

正解　(C)

・occupy	*v.* 佔用，佔據		・group	*v.* 集中，組合
・wastebasket	*n.* 垃圾桶		・plain	*a.* 素色的，素面的
・carpet	*n.* 地毯			

6

(A) The man is getting out of the car
(B) The man is walking quickly.
(C) The man is selling tabloids.
(D) The man has a cap on.

(A) 男子從車裡出來。
(B) 男子正快步行走。
(C) 男子在賣報紙。
(D) 男子戴著帽子。

正解　(D)

・get out of ~	從・出來		・tabloid	*n.* (八卦)小報
・cap	*n.*（有帽簷的）帽子			

7

(A) People are sitting under potted trees.
(B) There are many spotted trees.
(C) One man is on his feet.
(D) This is an outdoor park.

(A) 人們坐在盆栽樹下。
(B) 有許多有斑點的樹。
(C) 一位男士站著。
(D) 這是個戶外公園。

正解 **(A)**

・ potted　　*a.* 花盆栽種的　　　　・ spotted　*a.* 有斑點的
・ outdoor　 *a.* 戶外的

8

(A) The houses are each shaped very differently.
(B) There is a crow on the grass.
(C) Some houses are not suitable for living.
(D) There is a row of houses.

(A) 每間房子的形狀都不一樣。
(B) 草地上有一隻烏鴉。
(C) 有些房子不適合居住。
(D) 有一排房子並列著。

正解 **(D)**

・ shape　　*v.* 塑形，建造　　　　・ crow　*n.* 烏鴉
・ suitable　*a.* 適合的　　　　　　・ row　 *n.* 排，列

中　文　翻　譯　和　解　答

9

(A) She is putting newspapers in order
(B) This floor is very slippery.
(C) The woman is wallpapering.
(D) The woman is on a small rug.

(A) 她正依序擺放報紙。
(B) 地板非常滑。
(C) 女子正在黏貼壁紙。
(D) 女子站在小地毯上。

正解 **(D)**

· put ~ in order	按順序擺放	· slippery	*a.* 滑的，滑動的
· wallpaper	*v.* 黏貼壁紙	· rug	*n.* （小塊）地毯

10

(A) There is a table protruding from the wall.
(B) Liquid is spilling from the plastic cup.
(C) The door is open wide.
(D) A table is blocking a door

(A) 有張桌子從牆壁突出來。
(B) 液體從塑膠杯裡溢出。
(C) 門是敞開的。
(D) 有張桌子擋住了門。

正解 **(D)**

· protrude	*v.* 突出，伸出	· liquid	*n.* 液體
· spill	*v.* 潑灑	· plastic	*a.* 塑膠的
· block	*v.* 阻擋		

Part 2  CD 2 No. 4

| 中 文 翻 譯 | 解 答 和 單 字 |

11

How did this information get disclosed to the press?

(A) The printing office was closed.
(B) We sent the documents to the printers.
(C) Someone must have told them.

這個訊息是怎麼洩漏給媒體的？

(A) 這家印刷公司下班了。
(B) 我們把文件寄給印刷廠了。
(C) 一定是有人告訴他們。

正解 **(C)**

· disclose
 v. 揭發，洩露
· press
 n. 新聞界，媒體
· printing office
 印刷公司
· document
 n. 文件
· printer
 n. 印刷廠，印表機

12

Did your brother really start his own firm?

(A) We are firm on this offer
(B) Well, it's not completely his.
(C) Yes. He just started the engine and drove off

你弟弟真的自己開公司了嗎？

(A) 我們堅持這項報價。
(B) 嗯，並不是他一個人的。
(C) 是的，他剛發動引擎開車走了。

正解 **(B)**

· firm
 n. 公司，行號
· firm
 a. 堅定的，穩固的
· offer
 n. 出價，提議
· engine
 n. 引擎

13

Would you tell me the extension number?

(A) I have already extended it.
(B) I can't tell you when I'll get off work.
(C) I could connect you if you want.

可以告訴我分機號碼嗎？

(A) 我們已經把它延長了。
(B) 我沒辦法告訴你我何時會下班。
(C) 如果你要的話我可以幫你接通。

正解 **(C)**

· extension number
 分機號碼
· extend
 v. 延伸，擴展
· connect
 v. 連接，接通

| 中　文　翻　譯 | 解　答　和　單　字 |

14

Does this facility have proper emergency exits?

(A) Yes. There is one on each side.
(B) Sure. I will facilitate this project.
(C) No. I think that we have time.

這個場所有適當的緊急出口嗎？

(A) 是的，每邊各有一個。
(B) 當然，我會促成這個計畫。
(C) 沒有，我認為我們還有時間。

正解　**(A)**

・facility
　　n. (特定用途)場所，設施
・proper
　　a. 適當的，正確的
・emergency exit
　　緊急出口
・facilitate
　　v. 使容易，促進
・project
　　n. 計劃，企劃

15

What year did you found this organization?

(A) I found it two years ago.
(B) I founded it in 1980.
(C) He created it in 1999.

你何時成立這個組織？

(A) 我兩年前發現的。
(B) 我在1980年成立的。
(C) 他在1999年創立的。

正解　**(B)**

・found
　　v. 成立，創辦
・organization
　　n. 組織，機構
・create
　　v. 創造，產生

16

Did you like working at headquarters?

(A) No. I took half
(B) I like this branch better
(C) Well, maybe three-quarters.

你喜歡在總公司上班嗎？

(A) 不，我拿了一半。
(B) 我比較喜歡這間分公司。
(C) 嗯，或許四分之二。

正解　**(B)**

・headquarters
　　n. 總部，總公司
・branch
　　n. 分公司，分店

17

Do you think that merger will create a monopoly?

(A) I think they will merge.
(B) I guess a merger will happen.
(C) I bet it probably will.

你覺得那件合併案會造成壟斷嗎？
(A) 我覺得他們會合併。
(B) 我想會合併。
(C) 我確信很可能會。

正解 (C)

• merger
　n. 合併（案）
• monopoly
　n. 壟斷，獨占

18

Has the patent application been sent?

(A) I did it myself yesterday.
(B) I was not accepted.
(C) Of course, I save every cent.

專利申請書已經寄出去了嗎？
(A) 我昨天親自寄的。
(B) 我沒通過。
(C) 當然，我每一分錢都存了下來。

正解 (A)

• patent
　n. 專利，專賣（權）
• application
　n. 申請
• accept
　v. 接受，同意

19

I'm sorry, but have we been introduced?

(A) I don't think so.
(B) We were all sorry.
(C) I read the introduction.

對不起，我們彼此介紹過了嗎？
(A) 我想還沒有。
(B) 我們都感到很抱歉。
(C) 我看過序言了。

正解 (A)

• introduce
　v. 介紹，引進
• introduction
　n. 引言，緒論

中 文 翻 譯	解 答 和 單 字

20

Did you follow the procedure?

(A) Yes, I will.
(B) No, I didn't.
(C) Of course, you did.

正解 **(B)**

· procedure
  n. 程序

你有沒有按照程序？

(A) 是的，我會。
(B) 不，我並沒有。
(C) 當然，你有。

21

When did you get in?

(A) Just a little before you did.
(B) I'm going in tomorrow.
(C) I don't really want to.

正解 **(A)**

· get in
  到達

你何時到達的？

(A) 只比你早一點到。
(B) 我明天加入。
(C) 我不太想要。

22

Why don't you give me a call when you find out?

(A) I've never been better!
(B) At about 3 o'clock.
(C) Will do.

正解 **(C)**

· find out
  查明，發現

查明後請打電話給我，好嗎？

(A) 我從來沒這麼好過。
(B) 大約二點。
(C) 會的。

23

I asked you to make me a copy.

(A) It's on your desk.
(B) Thanks a lot.
(C) I'll need about four

我之前要你幫我弄一份副本。

(A) 放在你桌上。
(B) 多謝了。
(C) 我需要四份。

正解 **(A)**

・copy
　n. 副本，複製本，份數

24

Do you fit a medium?

(A) No, medium rare, please.
(B) Yes, I will fit out a new kitchen.
(C) Well, a large would be better

你能穿中號的嗎？

(A) 不，半熟。
(B) 是的，我會裝設新的廚房。
(C) 嗯，大號尺寸會比較好。

正解 **(C)**

・medium
　n. 中等，中號大小
・rare
　a. 煮得嫩的（帶血）
・medium rare
　半熟（__分熟）
・fit out
　裝備，設備

25

What did Mr Brown say about the error?

(A) He's doing just fine.
(B) He's writing a memo about it now.
(C) Mr Brown is the division manager

Brown先生對這失誤怎麼說？

(A) 他做得不錯。
(B) 他正在寫有關失誤的紀錄。
(C) Brown先生是部門經理。

正解 **(B)**

・error
　n. 錯誤，失誤，過失
・memo = memorandum
　n. 備忘錄，公司內部公文
・division
　n. 部門，部分

| 中　文　翻　譯 | 解　答　和　單　字 |

26

Have you ever heard this song before?

(A) Actually, it's one of my favorites.
(B) No, I don't sing that well.
(C) Yes, he is my son.

你曾聽過這首歌嗎？
(A) 實際上，它是我最喜愛的歌曲之一。
(B) 不，我唱得沒那麼好。
(C) 是的，他是我兒子。

正解 **(A)**

・favorite
　n. 最喜愛的東西（人）

27

Excuse me, could you direct me to the exit, please?

(A) Sure, it's over to the right.
(B) I'm not ready to leave yet.
(C) You can get in through there.

抱歉，請你告訴我出口怎麼走，好嗎？
(A) 當然，就在過去一點，靠右邊。
(B) 我還不準備離開。
(C) 你可以從那兒進來。

正解 **(A)**

・direct
　v. 給‥指路，指示方向
・exit
　n. 出口

28

You won't believe what I saw today!

(A) Tell me!
(B) But I didn't see you today.
(C) Well, you do believe!

你絕對不會相信我今天看到了什麼！
(A) 你快說啊！
(B) 但我今天沒看到你。
(C) 你真的相信！

正解 **(A)**

・believe
　v. 相信

29

Wow, things have really changed around here, haven't they?

(A) Yeah, you have been gone for a while, you know.
(B) No, we're quite comfortable here.
(C) I'm sorry we don't carry change.

哇！這裡改變了好多，不是嗎？
(A) 對呀！你已經離開好一陣子了。
(B) 不，我們在這兒很舒服。
(C) 對不起，我們沒帶零錢。

正解 **(A)**

- for a while 一會兒
- quite a while
  相當長一段時間
- all the while 這段時間
- once in a while
  偶爾，有時
- worth one's while
  值得某人做·
- comfortable
  a. 舒適的，輕鬆自在的
- change
  n. 零錢(沒有複數形)，改變

30

The computer seems to be broken.

(A) Thanks for fixing it.
(B) No, John broke it.
(C) Are you sure? You better double-check.

這台電腦似乎已經壞了。
(A) 謝謝你修好它。
(B) 不，John弄壞的。
(C) 確定嗎? 你最好再檢查一下。

正解 **(C)**

- fix
  v. 修理
- you better = you had better
  你最好·
- double-check
  v. 再檢查，複查

31

Can you help me find this book?

(A) Who's the author?
(B) Thanks, I just got it.
(C) It was founded a few years ago.

可以幫我找這本書嗎？
(A) 作者是誰？
(B) 謝謝，我剛找到。
(C) 它在幾年前就成立了。

正解 **(A)**

- author
  n. 作者，作家
- found
  v. 建立，興建，創辦，
  也是find的過去式

中 文 翻 譯	解 答 和 單 字

32

What's the recommended dosage?

(A) I don't like sausages.
(B) Once every eight hours.
(C) I recommend that Italian restaurant.

建議的劑量是多少？

(A) 我不喜歡香腸。
(B) 每八小時服用一次。
(C) 我推薦那家義大利餐廳。

正解 (B)

· recommend
  v. 介紹，推薦
· dosage
  n. 劑量，服用量
· sausage
  n. 香腸
· Italian restaurant
  義大利餐廳，義式餐廳

33

How much paper should I order?

(A) The usual.
(B) I read the paper this morning.
(C) No thanks, I'm full.

該訂多少紙張？

(A) 照往常的量。
(B) 我今天早上看了報紙。
(C) 不，謝謝，我飽了。

正解 (A)

· order
  v. 訂購，訂貨
· full
  a. 飽的

34

Who's going to replace Ms. Castro?

(A) Ms. Castro is not in at the moment.
(B) Would you like to leave a message?
(C) They're doing interviews now.

誰會來接替Castro女士？

(A) Castro女士現在不在。
(B) 你要留話嗎？
(C) 他們現在正在面試。

正解 (C)

· replace
  v. 取代，代替
· at the moment
  現在，此刻
· leave a message
  留言，留話
· interview
  n. 面試，訪談

35

How would you like to send this?

(A) Just these letters, please.
(B) First class, please.
(C) Please don't end it.

你這件東西要怎麼寄？

(A) 只有這些信，麻煩你。
(B) 請用快遞。
(C) 請不要終止它。

正解 (B)

· first class
　一流的，(郵政)快速郵件
　，(車廂，機位)頭等艙
· end
　v. 終止，結束

36

Did you actually pay for that?

(A) Don't you think it's worth it?
(B) That'll be 52 dollars, please.
(C) Cash or credit card?

你真的付錢了嗎？

(A) 你不認為值得嗎？
(B) 總共52元。
(C) 付現還是刷卡？

正解 (A)

· actually
　adv. 實際上
· credit
　n. 信用（卡）

37

One adult and one student ticket, please.

(A) I don't like watching cricket.
(B) No, I'm not a student.
(C) May I see your student ID, please?

請給我一張成人票、一張學生票。

(A) 我不喜歡看板球。
(B) 不，我不是學生。
(C) 請出示你的學生證。

正解 (C)

· cricket
　n. 板球

中 文 翻 譯　　　解 答 和 單 字

38

Where can I get some cash?

(A) There's an ATM around the corner
(B) I already threw out the trash.
(C) Thanks for lending me some.

我可以在哪兒換現金？

(A) 轉角有個提款機。
(B) 我已經把垃圾丟了。
(C) 謝謝你借我一些錢。

正解 **(A)**

• corner
　　n. 角落，轉角
• trash
　　n. 垃圾，廢物

39

How many people have arrived?

(A) There are 52 reservations.
(B) Why don't you check the guest book?
(C) They arrived a couple of minutes ago.

已經來了多少人？

(A) 有52個預約。
(B) 何不看看來賓簽到簿？
(C) 他們幾分鐘前才到。

正解 **(B)**

• reservation
　　n. 預約
• guest
　　n. 賓客，客人
• a couple of
　　一些，幾個，一對，一雙

40

Aren't you going to buy anything?

(A) No, nothing caught my eye.
(B) Yes, I spent so much money!
(C) Thanks, that was very thoughtful of you.

你不買東西嗎？

(A) 不，我沒看上任何東西。
(B) 是的，我已經花了好多錢。
(C) 謝謝，您太周到了。

正解 **(A)**

• catch ~ eye
　　引起 ·的注意
• thoughtful
　　a. 關心體貼的，費心的

聽　力　原　文　／　中　譯

Questions 41 through 43 refer to the following conversation.

M: It was only sprinkling this early morning, but it looks like the rain is really starting to come down.

W: How about putting the picnic lunch off until tomorrow? I'd think twice if I were you.

M: Yeah, you're probably right. I better call everyone and let them know. I'll do my best, but it's going to take some time.

W: I know it's a lot of work, but it needs to be finished by ten o'clock.

(男) 今天清晨只下毛毛雨，但現在看起來好像真的要下雨了。

(女) 把野餐延到明天如何？如果換成是我，我會仔細考慮。

(男) 也許你說的對，我最好打電話通知大家。我盡量做好，但得花點時間。

(女) 我知道很費事，但十點以前就得完成。

Word Bank

· sprinkling	*n.* 少許雨水，毛毛雨	· put ~ off	把 ·延期，把 ·改期
· picnic	*n.* 野餐	· postpone	*v.* 延期，延遲
· think twice	仔細考慮		

《題解篇》

中　文　翻　譯　和　解　答

41

What did they decide to do?

(A) Postpone the picnic
(B) Cancel the picnic
(C) Have a picnic
(D) Plan a picnic

他們決定做什麼？

(A) 將野餐延期
(B) 取消野餐
(C) 舉行野餐
(D) 安排野餐

正解 **(A)**

· postpone
　v. 延期，延續

42

According to the conversation, how was the weather earlier this morning?

(A) It was pouring.
(B) It was drizzling.
(C) It was showering.
(D) It was raining hard.

根據對話內容，今天一早天氣如何？

(A) 下傾盆大雨。
(B) 下毛毛細雨。
(C) 下陣雨。
(D) 下大雨。

正解 **(B)**

· pouring
　a. 傾盆大雨的
· drizzling
　a. 毛毛細雨的
· showering
　a. 陣雨的

43

When should the man notify everyone of the change?

(A) In the evening
(B) At night
(C) Until tomorrow
(D) In the morning

男士應該在什麼時候通知大家計劃改變？

(A) 在晚上
(B) 夜間
(C) 等到明天
(D) 上午中

正解 **(D)**

· notify
　v. 通知

Questions 44 through 46 refer to the following conversation.

W: Tell me a little bit about your past work.

M: Well, I worked with an advertising agency for two years. And it had clients that wanted to do television commercials. I can take a job from the initial concept all the way to the final bit of production.

W: Why do you want to change your job now? It's no picnic to work as a marketing manager.

M: Basically, I really feel I'm at this point in my career where I want to get into business management, and then I'll start working with people a lot more. I'm not quite sure how to achieve it.

(女) 請你談一談以前的工作。
(男) 我在一家廣告公司工作了兩年,有許多要做電視廣告的客戶。從最初的構想到製作的最後部份,我能夠完全負責。
(女) 為何你現在要換工作?當一個行銷經理並不輕鬆。
(男) 基本上,我真的覺得我的生涯到了這個時候,該要投入商業管理階層了,然後我會更常和他人一起工作。我並沒有把握要如何去達成。

Word Bank

• advertising agency	廣告公司	• client	*n.*	顧客,客戶;病人
• commercial	*n.* (電視、電台)廣告	• initial	*a.*	最初的,開始的
• bit	*n.* 部份	• production	*n.*	製作;生產
• no picnic	不輕鬆	• at this point		在這時候
• career	*n.* 生涯;事業	• achieve	*v.*	達到,成就

中　文　翻　譯　和　解　答

44

What did the man expect to do?

(A) To do television commercials.
(B) To work on an advertising project.
(C) To get into business management.
(D) To get a temporary job.

這男子希望做什麼？

(A) 做電視廣告。
(B) 做一個廣告企劃。
(C) 投入商業管理階層。
(D) 找一份暫時的工作。

正解 **(C)**

‧ temporary
a. 暫時的

45

What did the man do?

(A) He worked as a doctor.
(B) He worked in advertising.
(C) He was a marketing manager.
(D) He was a businessman.

這男子做過什麼工作？

(A) 他做過醫生。
(B) 他在廣告界做事。
(C) 他做過行銷經理。
(D) 他以前是生意人。

正解 **(B)**

46

What is the woman working on?

(A) A customers' survey
(B) A beauty contest
(C) A training program
(D) An interview with a candidate

這女子正在負責什麼工作？

(A) 顧客意見調查
(B) 選美比賽
(C) 培訓方案
(D) 面試一位應徵者

正解 **(D)**

‧ survey
n. 意見調查
‧ contest
n. 比賽
‧ candidate
n. 候選人，
應徵者

Questions 47 through 49 refer to the following conversation.

M: Have you got any information from Smith yet? You sent him the original copy of my report days ago. I think there's a mistake.

W: He's out of town and won't be back for another week as of today. Where is the mistake in your report?

M: In the introduction. I might be wrong, but I want to make sure.

W: Don't worry about it! It's much easier to correct mistakes at an early stage. Maybe you can ask his secretary when he comes back.

(男) 你有收到Smith的任何消息嗎？你幾天前就把我的報告原稿給他了。我覺得有個錯誤。

(女) 他到外地去了，還要再一個禮拜才會回來。你報告中的錯誤在哪兒？

(男) 在引言部份。我可能弄錯，但我要確定一下。

(女) 別擔心！在初期改正錯誤容易得多。或許等他回來再問他的秘書。

Word Bank

- original　　　***n.*** 原始的
- mistake　　　***n.*** 錯誤
- stage　　　　***n.*** 階段；時期
- secretary　　***n.*** 秘書
- introduction　***n.*** 導言；介紹

中 文 翻 譯 和 解 答

47

When will Smith be back?

(A) Within the week
(B) In a week
(C) After two weeks
(D) Today

Smith何時回來？

(A) 本週內
(B) 一星期後
(C) 兩週後
(D) 今天

正解 **(B)**

48

Where is the error?

(A) In the figures
(B) At the end of the report
(C) In the middle of the report
(D) In the beginning of the report

哪裡出錯？

(A) 數據方面
(B) 報告的結尾
(C) 報告的中間
(D) 報告的開頭

正解 **(D)**

・figures
　n. 數據，數字

49

Who is the woman?

(A) Smith's secretary
(B) The man's mother
(C) The man's coworker
(D) An usher

這位女士是誰？

(A) Smith的秘書
(B) 男士的母親
(C) 男士的同事
(D) 帶位員

正解 **(C)**

・coworker
　n. 同事
・usher
　n. 帶位員

Questions 50 through 52 refer to the following conversation.

M: Has the latest Business World magazine come in yet? I want to make sure our ad is in it. And I would like to order a back issue of Inside Business.

W: I'm sure a recent issue has. But you have to order back issues from the publishing company.

M: That's OK. Can you tell me how to contact the publisher?

W: Yes, that's no problem. I'll get the information you need from the Internet.

(男) 最新一期的「商業世界」雜誌來了沒？我要確認我們的廣告有刊登出來。同時，我想訂購「商業內幕」的過期雜誌。

(女) 我確定最新一期已經來了。但是，你要訂購過期雜誌，必須找出版社。

(男) 沒關係。可以告訴我怎麼連絡出版社嗎？

(女) 沒問題。我會上網找你要的資料。

Word Bank

- back issue　　　　過期雜誌
- inside　　　　　*n.* 內部消息；*a.* 內幕的
- publishing company 出版公司
- contact　*v.* 聯絡；接觸
- publisher　*n.* 出版商(社)
- Internet　*n.* 網路

中　文　翻　譯　和　解　答

50

What does the man want to do?

(A) Check the magazine for an advertisement
(B) Order a magazine subscription
(C) Have copies of a magazine made
(D) Place an advertisement in a magazine

男士要做什麼？

(A) 確認雜誌上的廣告
(B) 訂閱雜誌
(C) 影印雜誌
(D) 在雜誌上登廣告

正解 **(A)**

• subscription
  n. 訂閱

51

What does the man want to order?

(A) An earlier copy of Inside Business
(B) A back issue of Business World
(C) A current issue of Business World
(D) A current copy of Inside

男士要訂購什麼？

(A) 舊的「商業內幕」
(B) 過期的「商業世界」
(C) 當期的「商業世界」
(D) 當期的「商業內幕」

正解 **(A)**

52

How will the woman get the information for the man?

(A) By going online
(B) By contacting the publisher
(C) By ordering a magazine
(D) By advertising in a magazine

這女士如何替男士取得資訊？

(A) 上網
(B) 電話聯繫
(C) 訂雜誌
(D) 在雜誌登廣告

正解 **(A)**

Questions 53 through 55 refer to the following conversation.

W: The merger proposal from Intertech Incorporated is unacceptable. They've undervalued our company by half. It looks like we're not getting the merger contract.

M: I thought we were about ready to sign. They probably thought we'd just accept their first offer. We should send them a counter offer telling them we want more shares.

W: They're a big company, though. I don't know if we can get much more out of them than this.

M: We have to find out what their bottom line is, and hold out for a fair deal.

(女) Intertech集團的合併案令人無法接受。他們低估了我們公司一半的價值。看來我們無法拿到合併合約了。

(男) 我還以為我們準備簽約了。他們或許認為我們會接受他們第一次的出價。我們應該另外出價，告訴他們我們要更多的股份。

(女) 但是他們是大公司。我不知道是否能得到比現在更高的價錢。

(男) 我們得了解他們的底線，同時堅持要求公平的交易。

Word Bank

• merger	***n.*** (公司)合併	• proposal	***n.*** 計劃，建議
• incorporated = Inc	***a.*** 股份有限的	• unacceptable	***a.*** 不能接受的
• undervalue	***v.*** 低估	• probably	***adv.*** 可能地
• offer	***n.*** 出價，提議	• counter	***a.*** 相反的
• bottom line	底線	• fair deal	公平的交易

中　文　翻　譯　和　解　答

53

Why is the merger proposal unacceptable?

(A) It does not reflect the company's true value.
(B) It is Intertech's first offer.
(C) Intertech Incorporated may not give much more.
(D) The company's stock is too expensive.

為何這項合併案無法接受？

(A) 未反映公司真正的價值。
(B) 它是Intertech的第一次出價。
(C) Intertech集團可能不會出高價。
(D) 這家公司的股價太高。

正解 **(A)**

‧ reflect
　n. 反映，反射

54

Why isn't the speakers' company going to get the contract?

(A) Intertech didn't get any good offers.
(B) They were not ready to sign in time.
(C) Intertech got a better deal somewhere else.
(D) Both companies didn't come to an agreement.

為何談話者的公司無法拿到合約？

(A) Intertech沒得到好價錢。
(B) 他們未及時準備好簽約。
(C) Intertech在別處得到更好的交易。
(D) 兩家公司未達成協議。

正解 **(D)**

‧ offer
　n. 出價，價錢
‧ agreement
　n. 協議

55

How did the man feel about the merger?

(A) It is unalterable.
(B) It is highly profitable.
(C) It is unjust.
(D) It is unlawful.

男士對合併案感覺如何？

(A) 完全無法變更。
(B) 它獲利很高。
(C) 它是不合理的。
(D) 它是不合法的。

正解 **(C)**

‧ unalterable
　a. 不可改變的
‧ profitable
　a. 有利可圖的
‧ unjust
　a. 不合理的

Questions 56 through 58 refer to the following conversation.

M: I have some questions about your sales report . Do you have time this afternoon? And we are meeting to discuss how to deal with the problem of executing it on a pretty tight budget.

W: I'm sorry, but I have to prepare all this afternoon for a big promotion meeting this evening. How does tomorrow afternoon sound?

M: Actually, I'd like to get some details, so I'll need a little bit more time. Why don't we talk over lunch tomorrow?

W: Great. I'll ask you for your opinion.

(男) 我對你的業務報告有些疑問,你今天下午有空嗎?同時,我們要開會討論如何用很緊的預算,來處理執行的問題。

(女) 抱歉,我整個下午得要準備晚上的促銷會議。明天下午可以嗎?

(男) 實際上,我想了解一些細節,所以需要多一點時間。我們明天邊用午餐邊談如何?

(女) 太好了!我會請教您的意見。

Word Bank

- execute　*v.* 執行
- detail　*n.* 細節
- budget　*n.* 預算
- bother　*v.* 打擾

中　文　翻　譯　和　解　答

56

What does the woman want to do first?

(A) Take lunch
(B) Prepare the evening's meeting
(C) Ask the man for his opinion
(D) Revise her sales report

這位女士想要先做什麼？

(A) 吃午餐。
(B) 準備晚上的會議。
(C) 請教男士意見。
(D) 修正她的業務報告。

正解 **(B)**

・revise
v. 修正，修訂

57

What kind of questions does the man have?

(A) Personal
(B) Unrelated
(C) In-depth
(D) Brief

男士有何種疑問？

(A) 個人的
(B) 無關的
(C) 深入的
(D) 簡短的

正解 **(C)**

・unrelated
a. 無關的
・in-depth
a. 深入的
・brief
a. 簡短的

58

At what stage is the preparation of the promotion meeting?

(A) Finished
(B) Well prepared
(C) Preliminary
(D) Final

促銷會議的準備到了什麼階段？

(A) 完成了
(B) 充分準備了
(C) 初步階段
(D) 最後階段

正解 **(C)**

・promotion
n. 促銷
・organize
v. 安排，籌辦

Questions 59 through 61 refer to the following conversation.

W: Of the 15 members of the Board of Directors, eight have said that they would support your proposal.

M: And what of the others? I need at least a two-thirds majority to get anything passed.

W: The others won't say at all. I don't think we'll find out which way they'll vote beforehand.

M: I'll manage to persuade all of the members into backing my proposal.

(女) 董事會十五位成員當中，有八位表示他們會支持你的提案。

(男) 其他人呢？我至少需要三分之二的票才能通過。

(女) 其他人根本不肯說。我想不可能事先知道他們的意願。

(男) 我會設法說服所有成員支持我的提案。

Word Bank

· board of directors	董事會	· majority	*n.* 多數，大半
· beforehand	*adv.* 事先，預先	· at least	至少
· persuade	*v.* 說服…，使…相信	· argument	*n.* 論點

59

How many votes are needed to support the man's proposal?

(A) 8 votes
(B) At least one more
(C) At least 10
(D) All 15 votes

男士需要多少票來支持他的提案？

(A) 八票
(B) 至少再多一票
(C) 至少十票
(D) 所有的十五票

正解 **(C)**

· majority
  n. 大多數

60

Who is the man?

(A) A supporter of the proposal
(B) The chairman of the Board
(C) The company's founder
(D) The author of the proposal

男士是誰？

(A) 提案的支持者
(B) 董事長
(C) 公司創辦人
(D) 提案的撰寫人

正解 **(D)**

· founder
  n. 創辦人，創立者

61

Who is the woman?

(A) The man's colleague
(B) A director of the company
(C) The general president of the company
(D) A cleaner

女士是誰？

(A) 男士的同事。
(B) 公司的董事。
(C) 公司的總經理。
(D) 清潔工。

正解 **(A)**

· colleague
  n. 同事
· director
  n. 董事，主任

Questions 62 through 64 refer to the following conversation.

M: Hi, I need a medical exam. How far in advance would I have to make an appointment?

W: It all depends. If it's just a general checkup, a week in advance is fine. For other procedures, call at least two weeks before.

M: Ok, thanks. I'll check my schedule and give you a call to set up a date for the physical. By the way, do you know where I could find cold medicine?

W: That would be in our pharmaceutical department over there.

(男) 嗨！我要作體檢，我必須提前多久預約？

(女) 看情形。如果只是一般的健康檢查，一週前就可以。至於其他的程序，至少兩週前就要打電話。

(男) 好，謝謝。我看一下我的行程，再打電話預約體檢的日期。順便請問，你知道在哪裡可以買到感冒藥嗎？

(女) 在那邊的藥品部門。

Word Bank

· in advance		預先，提前	· appointment	*n.* 預約，約定
· depend	*v.*	根據…而定，取決於…	· general	*a.* 一般的
· checkup	*n.*	體檢，健康檢查	· procedure	*n.* 程序，手續
· at least		至少	· schedule	*n.* 時間表，進度表
· dentist	*n.*	牙醫	· medical	*n.* 體檢
· pharmaceutical	*a.*	藥劑的		

中　文　翻　譯　和　解　答

62

Why does the man want to make an appointment?

(A) He wants to have a medical checkup.
(B) He wants to see a dentist.
(C) He wants to visit the pharmacy.
(D) He wants a new schedule.

為何男子要預約？

(A) 他要作體檢。
(B) 他要看牙醫。
(C) 他要去藥房。
(D) 他要新的時間表。

正解 **(A)**

・ dentist
  n. 牙醫

63

What could the woman's occupation be?

(A) A waitress
(B) A doctor
(C) A sales check
(D) A receptionist

女士的職業可能是什麼？

(A) 女服務生
(B) 醫生
(C) 售貨員
(D) 櫃檯人員

正解 **(D)**

・ occupation
  n. 職業
・ clerk
  n. 店員
・ receptionist
  n. 櫃檯人員，
　　接待員

64

What will the man do first when he needs a checkup?

(A) Go to the pharmaceutical department.
(B) Go on a date with the woman.
(C) Buy cold medicine.
(D) Check his schedule and set a date.

男士要作體檢的話，他要先做什麼？

(A) 去藥品部門。
(B) 和女士約會。
(C) 買感冒藥。
(D) 查行程並預約日期。

正解 **(D)**

Questions 65 through 67 refer to the following conversation.

M: I heard you got into a car crash yesterday morning. Are you all right?

W: The driver and I are fine, thanks. The only damage was done to the car.

M: You seem very nervous after the car crash. You should take a well-earned rest a couple of days from your work.

W: I'd love to but I really can't. I have to start a new assignment.

(男) 聽說你昨天早上發生車禍。你還好嗎？

(女) 駕駛和我都還好，謝謝。只有車輛損壞了。

(男) 車禍之後，你似乎顯得很緊張。你應該暫停幾天工作，好好休息。

(女) 我很想休息，但真的不行。我必須開始著手新的任務。

Word Bank

• crash	*n.* 碰撞，衝撞	• damage	*n.* 損傷，破壞
• well-earned	*a.* 應得的	• car crash	車禍
• assignment	*n.* 分派的工作；作業	• a couple of	幾個

中　文　翻　譯　和　解　答

65

What was damaged the most?

(A) The car
(B) The woman
(C) The car driver
(D) The auto mechanic

什麼受損最嚴重？

(A) 車子
(B) 女士
(C) 車輛駕駛
(D) 修車技師

正解 **(A)**

• mechanic
  n. 技工

66

How does the woman seem?

(A) depressed
(B) disappointed
(C) excited
(D) emotionally tense

女士看來情況如何？

(A) 沮喪的
(B) 失望的
(C) 興奮的
(D) 情緒緊張的

正解 **(D)**

• depressed
  a. 沮喪的
• emotionally
  adv. 情緒上的
• tense
  a. 緊張的

67

What does the man suggest the woman do?

(A) Start a new job
(B) Rest for a few days
(C) Repair her car
(D) Forget about the car accident

男士建議女士做什麼？

(A) 開始新的工作
(B) 休息幾天
(C) 修理她的車子
(D) 忘了車禍

正解 **(B)**

• accident
  n. 意外

Questions 68 through 70 refer to the following conversation.

M: When are you going to get back to me on that proposal? And have you come to a decision on it?

W: Didn't you get the e-mail I sent you? If you agree to our changes, we would be more than happy to accept.

M: My computer has been down since yesterday. I don't think your changes will be a problem.

W: That would be a big help.

(男) 你何時可以回覆我那項企劃案？你作出決定了嗎？

(女) 你沒收到我給你的電子郵件嗎？如果你同意我們的變動，我們比較樂於接受。

(男) 我的電腦從昨天就壞了。我想你們的變動不是問題。

(女) 那真是幫了大忙。

Word Bank

- decision　　*n.* 決定
- accept　　*v.* 接受
- proposal　　　*n.* 企劃案，求婚
- make a decision　　做決定

中　文　翻　譯　和　解　答

68

What does the man want from the woman?

(A) To get married
(B) To do him a favor
(C) To tell him of her decision
(D) To tell her company to make a decision

男士要女士做什麼？

(A) 結婚
(B) 幫他忙
(C) 把她的決定告訴他
(D) 要她的公司做決定

正解 **(C)**

· decision
　n. 決定

69

Why didn't the man get a response from the woman?

(A) His computer was broken.
(B) He doesn't use e-mail.
(C) The woman didn't send the e-mail.
(D) He didn't offer the proposal.

為何男士沒收到女士的回答？

(A) 他的電腦壞了。
(B) 他沒使用電子郵件。
(C) 女士沒寄出電子郵件。
(D) 他沒提出企劃案。

正解 **(A)**

· response
　n. 反應；答案

70

How about the proposal?

(A) It has no problem.
(B) It'll be revised.
(C) No one will agree on it.
(D) The woman will negate it.

這項企劃案如何？

(A) 沒有問題。
(B) 將被修改。
(C) 沒有人會贊同。
(D) 女士將否定它。

正解 **(B)**

· revise
　v. 修訂，修改
· negate
　v. 否定；取消

Part 4 　CD 2　No. 8

Questions 71 through 73 refer to the following announcement.

Attention, all passengers. Thank you for riding W. S. Ferries. We will be arriving in the harbor of Nanaimo shortly, about ten minutes ahead of schedule. We would like to request that all passengers with vehicles take this time now to return to your vehicles and prepare to disembark. However, please do not start vehicle engines until instructed to do so by ferry personnel. We would also like to ask all bicycle passengers to be prepared to disembark, as bicycles will leave before automobiles. Walk-on passengers will disembark through the left-hand exit on the main passenger deck. Thank you.

請參考以下的廣播：

　　各位旅客，請注意。感謝您搭乘W.S.渡輪。我們很快就會抵達Nanaimo港口，大概比預定行程提早了十分鐘。我們要請所有乘坐交通工具的旅客，利用現在這段時間，回到自己的交通工具內，準備上岸。請聽從渡輪服務人員的指示，再發動汽機車引擎。我們也要請所有騎腳踏車的旅客準備上岸，因為腳踏車會在汽車之前先上岸。徒步的旅客，請您從乘客主甲板左邊的出口下船。謝謝各位。

Word Bank

• attention	*n.*	注意（力）	• passenger	*n.*	乘客，旅客
• ride	*v.*	乘坐	• ferry	*n.*	渡輪
• harbor	*n.*	港口	• shortly	*adv.*	馬上，很快地
• ahead of schedule		比預定時間提早	• vehicle	*n.*	車輛，運載工具
• disembark	*v.*	上岸，登陸	• engine	*n.*	引擎，發動機
• instruct	*v.*	指示，指導	• personnel	*n.*	人事，（全體）員工
• automobile	*n.*	汽車	• exit	*n.*	出口
• deck	*n.*	甲板			

中　文　翻　譯　和　解　答

71

When should passengers with cars return to their cars?

(A) 10 minutes before landing
(B) 10 minutes ahead of schedule
(C) Immediately after the announcement
(D) After instructed to do so by ferry personnel

駕車的旅客應該何時回到車上？

(A) 登陸前十分鐘
(B) 比預定行程提前十分鐘
(C) 聽到廣播之後
(D) 在渡輪人員指示之後

正解 **(C)**

• announcement
  n. 宣佈，廣播

72

Who will be allowed to leave before cars?

(A) People on bicycles
(B) People who are not on the passenger deck
(C) People with luggage
(D) People with small children

誰可以在車輛通行前先下船？

(A) 騎腳踏車的人
(B) 不在乘客甲板上的人
(C) 拿行李的乘客
(D) 帶小孩的乘客

正解 **(A)**

• allowed **a.** 允許的，獲准的
• luggage **n.** 行李

73

Who will leave the boat on the left side of the main passenger deck?

(A) People with bicycles
(B) People on foot
(C) People with large packages
(D) Ferry personnel

誰要從乘客主甲板的左邊出口下船？

(A) 有腳踏車的人
(B) 走路的人
(C) 有大件行李的人
(D) 渡輪的人員

正解 **(B)**

• on foot
  步行，徒步
• package
  n. 包裹
• ferry personnel
  渡輪上的工作人員

Questions 74 through 76 refer to the following speech.

I find it hard to express just how honored I feel to be standing before all of you today and receiving this award. If someone had told me ten years ago that people would value my research and work in the field of statistics to this extent, I really don't think I would have believed them. I have always applied myself to my research only because I am so interested in the maths and the theory involved. So as you thank me for just being who I am, I would like to thank you all for that support.

請參考以下的致詞：

今天能夠站在各位面前，接受這份獎項，我真的難以表達我感到多麼榮幸。如果有人十年前對我說，人們會重視我在統計學領域這範圍所從事的研究工作，我真的不敢相信。我一直專心致力於我的研究，只因為我對數學和其相關的理論非常感興趣。所以當你們向我的所作所為致謝，我也想感謝各位對我的支持。

Word Bank

• express	*v.* 表達	• honored	*a.* 覺得光榮的
• award	*n.* 獎，獎金，獎品	• value	*v.* 重視，珍惜
• research	*n.* 研究	• statistics	*n.* 統計（學），統計數字
• extent	*n.* 程度，範圍	• apply oneself to ~	致力於～，專心於～
• math	*n.* 數學（＝mathematics）	• theory	*n.* 理論
• involved	*a.* 相關的，涉入的	• support	*n.* 支持，贊助

中 文 翻 譯 和 解 答

74

Why is this person giving a speech?

此人為何要致詞？

正解 **(C)**

(A) The person is retiring
(B) The person got a promotion
(C) The person has been awarded a prize
(D) The person is introducing someone very famous

(A) 此人要退休了
(B) 此人獲得升遷
(C) 此人獲頒獎項
(D) 此人正在介紹某位知名人士

・award
　v. 得獎，頒獎
・prize
　n. 獎品，獎狀

75

Who is giving this speech?

什麼人在演講？

正解 **(C)**

(A) A librarian
(B) A company president
(C) A researcher
(D) A novelist

(A) 一位圖書館員
(B) 一位公司總裁
(C) 一位研究人員
(D) 一位小說家

・give this speech
　致詞，演講
・librarian
　n. 圖書館員
・president
　n. 總裁，總經理，董事長

76

What does the speaker specialize in?

這位致詞者專門研究什麼？

正解 **(B)**

(A) Numerology
(B) Statistics
(C) Strategy
(D) Evolution

(A) 數字學
(B) 統計學
(C) 戰略學
(D) 淨化學

・specialize
　v. 專門研究，專修
・strategy
　n. 戰略(學)
・theory
　n. 理論，學說

Questions 77 through 79 refer to the following talk.

Good evening, and welcome to tonight's edition of **Finance in Review**. Tonight we will be talking to Edward Richardson, who is the head of the Metropolitan Banking Group, as well as a member of the board of trustees for Anarco Steel Corporation. He has received the Jackson Award for excellence in the field of economics for his explanations of the economic effects of globalization on medium-sized corporations. Tonight he will be discussing recent important changes in the global economy.

請參考以下的談話：

　　大家晚安，歡迎來到今晚所播出的「財經評論」。今晚我們將與Edward Richardson對談，他是大都會銀行團的負責人，也是Anarco鋼鐵公司的理事。關於全球化經濟效益對中型企業造成的影響，他所做的論述精闢卓越，讓他獲頒Jackson大獎。今晚，他要來談談最近全球經濟的重大改變。

Word Bank

· edition	**n.** 版本，版次	· finance	**n.** 財經，金融
· review	**n.** 評論	· head	**n.** 負責人
· metropolitan	**n.** 大都會，城市	· as well as	也是，亦如
· member of the board	**n.** 理事，董事	· trustee	**n.** 信託公司
· corporation	**n.** 公司	· excellence	**n.** 卓越，優良（表現）
· field	**n.** 領域，範圍	· economics	**n.** 經濟（學）
· explanation	**n.** 解釋，闡述	· economic effect	經濟效益
· globalization	**n.** 全球化	· medium	**a.** 中等的
· recent	**a.** 最近的，近來的	· global	**a.** 全球的，球形的

中 文 翻 譯 和 解 答

77

What is Edward Richardson the head of?

(A) A banking group
(B) A steel company
(C) A unniversity of economics department
(D) A medium-sized company

Edward Richardson是哪個單位的負責人？

(A) 一個銀行團
(B) 一家鋼鐵公司
(C) 大學經濟系
(D) 一家中型公司

正解 **(A)**

· banking group
　銀行團
· steel
　n. 鋼鐵

78

What was Edward Richardson given an award for?

(A) His explanations of his company.
(B) His excitement about politics.
(C) His appearance on the show **Finance in Review**.
(D) His ideas on the effects of globalization.

Edward Richardson為何獲頒獎項？

(A) 他對其公司的說明。
(B) 他對政治的激情。
(C) 他在「財經評論」節目上露臉。
(D) 他對全球化影響的概念。

正解 **(D)**

· excitement
　n. 興奮，激動
· politics
　n. 政治（學）
· appearance
　n. 出現，外表

79

What will the award-winner be talking about on the show?

(A) Finance in Review
(B) economics
(C) recent economic changes
(D) globalization

得獎者將在節目中談論什麼？

(A) 財經評論
(B) 經濟學
(C) 最近的經濟變化
(D) 全球化

正解 **(C)**

· award-winner
　n. 獲獎者
· show
　n. 節目(電視或廣播)

Questions 80 through 82 refer to the following annoucement.

May I have your attention please; this is your captain speaking. We are currently experiencing quite a bit of turbulence due to a tropical storm due east of our flight route. There is nothing to be alarmed about, as we should be flying past this shortly. In the meantime, however, as it will be bumpy, please remain seated with your seatbelts fastened and please turn off all electronic devices. Flight attendants must also be seated at this time. They will be of assistance to you in just a few moments. Thank you.

請參考以下的廣播：

　　各位旅客請注意：這是機長廣播。由於熱帶暴風雨接近我們航線的東方，我們現在正穿越些微亂流。請大家不用驚慌，我們應該很快就會通過。因為這段期間會有顛簸，請各位在座位上坐好，繫上安全帶，並請關掉所有電子器材。空服員現在也務必回座。他們將於數分鐘後，繼續為您服務。謝謝各位。

Word Bank

• captain	*n.* 機長，船長，艦長		• currently	*adv.* 當前地
• experience	*v.* 經歷，體驗		• turbulence	*n.* 亂流
• due to ~	由於…		• tropical storm	熱帶暴風雨
• due	*a.* 預期的，應到達的，該發生的		• alarmed	*a.* 恐慌的，驚慌的
• past	*prep.* 越過		• shortly	*adv.* 不久，很快
• in the meantime	同時		• bumpy	*a.* 不平的，顛簸的
• seatbelt	*n.* 安全帶		• fasten	*v.* 固定
• turn off	關掉		• device	*n.* 設備，裝置
• flight attendant	空服員		• assistance	*n.* 幫助，協助

中 文 翻 譯 和 解 答

80

Who is being addressed?

(A) A ship captain
(B) Airport personnel
(C) Train passengers
(D) Cabin crew

聽這段話的人有誰？

(A) 船長
(B) 機場人員
(C) 火車乘客
(D) 機艙人員

正解 **(D)**

81

How long will the current situation continue?

(A) It is unknown.
(B) For a short time.
(C) For hours.
(D) Until the storm stops.

氣流的狀況會持續多久？

(A) 無法得知。
(B) 持續一小段時間。
(C) 數小時之久。
(D) 直到暴風雨停止。

正解 **(B)**

・current
　n. 氣流，潮流
・continue
　v. 持續，繼續

82

What must the listeners do?

(A) Sit down
(B) Fasten people in
(C) Stop serving meals
(D) Assist the speaker

聽者必須做什麼？

(A) 坐下
(B) 把人綁進來
(C) 停止供餐
(D) 協助講者

正解 **(A)**

・listener
　n. 聽者，聽眾
・speaker
　n. 講者，演講者

Questions 83 through 85 refer to the following voice report.

An unexpected windstorm hit the south Puget Sound region early yesterday morning, knocking down power lines and causing blackouts in many parts of Greater King County. Winds of up to 40 miles per hour sent tree limbs flying into storefront throughout downtown Seattle, forcing many small business owners to close down as early as 11:00 a.m.

Possibly most upsetting was the extremely low voter turnout for the City Council election brought about by the hazardous weather conditions. City officials are debating whether to allow late absentee ballots due to the unprecedented election day storm.

請參考以下的語音報導：

昨天清晨，一場毫無預警的暴風侵襲了 Puget Sound 的南部地區，吹倒了電纜線，造成 Greater King 郡的許多地方停電。時速高達40英哩的強風，颳起整個西雅圖市區的許多樹枝，砸進商店櫥窗，也迫使許多小店家老闆在早上11點就提早打烊。或許最令人困擾的是，由於惡劣的天候，造成市議會選舉的投票率偏低。市府官員正在討論，是否讓選舉當天因史無前例的暴風而未能投票的選民，再次投票。

Word Bank

· unexpected	*a.* 未料到的，無預期的	· windstorm	*n.* 暴風
· region	*n.* 地區	· blackout	*n.* 停電
· limb	*n.* (樹的)枝幹，(人的)四肢	· storefront	*n.* 店面
· force	*v.* 逼迫，迫使	· owner	*n.* 所有權人，(店家)老闆
· upsetting	*a.* 令人困擾的，難過的	· extremely	*adv.* 非常地，極為
· voter	*n.* 投票者，選民	· turnout	*n.* (集會之)出席人數
· election	*n.* 選舉	· hazardous	*a.* 危險的，冒險的
· debate	*v.* 辯論，討論	· absentee	*n.* 缺席者
· ballot	*n.* 投票(總數)，選票	· unprecedented	*a.* 史無前例的
· storm	*n.* 暴風(雨)		

中 文 翻 譯 和 解 答

83

What happened in the south Puget Sound region?

(A) An anti-government demonstration
(B) Flooding
(C) A windstorm
(D) A store robbery

在 Puget Sound 南部地區發生了什麼事？

(A) 反政府示威遊行
(B) 淹水
(C) 暴風
(D) 商店搶劫

正解 **(C)**

- anti-government
  n. 反政府
- demonstration
  n. 展示，示威，發表
- flooding
  n. 洪水，泛濫
- robbery
  n. 搶劫（案）

84

What time of the day did the problem begin?

(A) Early evening
(B) Early morning
(C) Midday
(D) Midnight

問題發生在當天什麼時間？

(A) 傍晚
(B) 清晨
(C) 中午
(D) 午夜

正解 **(B)**

- midday
  n. 中午，正午
- midnight
  n. 午夜，半夜

85

What event was interrupted?

(A) The business of small transportations
(B) The electric company's daily work
(C) People's use of water
(D) The election

什麼事件受到了最嚴重的干擾？

(A) 小型運輸業務
(B) 電力公司的日常作業
(C) 人們的用水
(D) 選舉

正解 **(D)**

- interrupt
  v. 干擾，打岔
- transportation
  n. 運輸，交通

Questions 86 through 88 refer to the following talk.

Your attention, please. Flight 177 is overbooked, so we are offering a free round-trip ticket to any of our Asian destinations for any passengers who can voluntarily give up their seats on this flight and fly out on tomorrow's 7:20 p.m. flight instead. If you are interested in this offer, please come to the ticket counter now. Again, please note that the departure gate for TGA Flight 177 bound for Bangkok has been changed. Passengers who are boarding Flight 177, please come to gate 20B. Boarding will now commence in about half an hour. Thank you for your cooperation.

請參考以下的廣播：

各位請注意：177班機因為超額訂位，如有任何旅客願意自動放棄本班次的機位，改搭明天晚上7:20的班機，我們將提供給您免費來回機票一張，可以飛往我們在亞洲地區的任一終點站。如果您有興趣，請立刻到票務櫃檯來。再次請您注意，TGA飛往曼谷的177班機，登機門已經更改。搭乘177班機的旅客，請前往20B登機門，再過半小時即將開始登機。謝謝您的合作。

Word Bank

• overbook	*v.* 超額預定	• round-trip	往返旅程
• destination	*n.* 目的地	• voluntarily	*adv.* 自願地
• ticket counter	票務櫃檯	• bound for	前往
• boarding	*n.* 登機	• commence	*v.* 開始

中 文 翻 譯 和 解 答

86

What do passengers have to do to get a free flight ?

(A) Flight a lot and collect more miles.
(B) Go to the ticket counter within 10 minutes.
(C) Give up their seat on Flight 177.
(D) Choose an Asian destination.

乘客必須做什麼才能獲得免費機票？

(A) 經常搭乘並累積哩程。
(B) 十分鐘內前往票務櫃台。
(C) 放棄177班機上的座位。
(D) 選擇一個亞洲的目的地。

正解 **(C)**

· collect
 v. 積聚

87

What has been changed?

(A) The flight number
(B) The flight time
(C) The departure gate
(D) The ticket prices

何者有所變更？

(A) 班機號碼
(B) 班機時間
(C) 離境登機門
(D) 票價

正解 **(C)**

· departure
 n. 啟程，離開

88

When will boarding start?

(A) In 20 minutes
(B) In 30 minutes
(C) At 7:20 p.m.
(D) At 7:50 p.m.

何時開始登機？

(A) 二十分鐘後
(B) 三十分鐘後
(C) 7:20 p.m.
(D) 7:50 p.m.

正解 **(B)**

· boarding
 n. 登機

Questions 89 through 91 refer to the following speech.

Last week, our accounting department released our company's quarterly report. As many of you already know, we were pleasantly surprised to learn that last quarter's profits increased by almost 15 percent! The management would like to personally thank everyone for their hard and diligent work by hosting a company-wide party at the Brew Haus Restaurant next Friday at 6:00 p.m. All food and drink will be complimentary until 9:00 p.m., and spouses and children are welcome. Once again, thank you for all your hard work. See you all on Friday!

請參考以下的致詞：

　　上個星期，我們會計部門的季報表已經出爐了。正如你們很多人所知，我們上一季的獲利增加到將近15%！我們都很驚喜。經營團隊要親自感謝各位的辛勞，我們將在下星期五晚上六點，於Brew Haus餐廳舉辦全公司的派對。所有餐飲都免費招待，一直供應到晚上九點，歡迎各位攜帶家眷子女一起來同樂。再次感謝大家的努力。我們星期五見囉！

Word Bank

· release	*v.* 公佈，發行，釋放	· quarterly	*a.* 按季的，每季的
· pleasantly	*adv.* 令人愉快地	· host	*v.* 主辦，主持
· complimentary	*a.* 免費的	· spouse	*n.* 配偶

中 文 翻 譯 和 解 答

89

Why is this company throwing a party?

(A) The manager of the company is retiring.
(B) The company's revenues increased by 15 percent.
(C) To thank the accounting department for the quarterly report.
(D) To show appreciation for an increase in company profits.

公司為何舉辦派對？

(A) 公司經理要退休。
(B) 公司的總營收增加15%。
(C) 感謝會計部門的季報表。
(D) 對公司增加獲利表達謝意。

正解 **(D)**

• revenue
  n. 收入，營收

90

Who may attend the party?

(A) Employees and clients
(B) Employees and their families
(C) Employees only
(D) Employees and celebrities

什麼人可以來參加派對？

(A) 員工和客戶
(B) 員工和家屬
(C) 只有員工
(D) 員工和顯要

正解 **(B)**

• celebrity
  n. 名人，名流

91

How many times is the report released every year?

(A) Once a year
(B) Once half a year
(C) Two times a quarter
(D) Four times a year

報告每年公佈幾次？

(A) 一年一次
(B) 半年一次
(C) 一季兩次
(D) 一年四次

正解 **(D)**

• release
  v. 發行，公佈

Questions 92 through 94 refer to the following talk.

Hello and welcome to Total Health. My name is Dana. I'll be your fitness consultant today. First of all, I need to make sure that all of you have read and signed the health release form. You cannot use the facilities until this has been signed. Next, we'll get you started on your fitness files. You can use this to record all of your vital statistics like weight, blood pressure, etc. And, it can help you keep track of your workout regimen. Then, we'll get you acquainted with all of the machines in the weight room. If you have any questions, please feel free to ask me at any time.

請參考以下的說話：

　　歡迎來到全方位健康中心。我叫Dana，是你們今天的健身顧問。首先我必須確定，你們每個人都看過這份健康調查表並且簽了名。一定要簽過之後，才能使用健身器材。接下來我們要為大家建立健康檔案。這份檔案將紀錄你所有重要的數據資料，像是體重、血壓等等。同時，它能幫助你掌握你的健身控管。然後我們要讓各位熟悉舉重室裡所有的機器。如果您有任何疑問，歡迎隨時來找我。

Word Bank

- fitness consultant　　健身顧問，健身諮詢師
- health release form　健康調查表
- record　*v.* 記錄
- statistics　*n.* 統計數字，統計資料
- blood pressure　血壓
- workout　*n.* 鍛鍊，健身，運動
- get ~ acquainted with　使熟悉
- first of all　首先
- facilities　*n.* 設施
- vital　*a.* 重要的
- weight　*n.* 重量
- keep track of　了解…的動態
- regimen　*n.* 控制

中　文　翻　譯　和　解　答

92

Where is this talk taking place?

這段話是在哪兒所說的？

正解 **(C)**

(A) At a camp
(B) At a hospital
(C) At a health club
(D) At a school

(A) 在營地
(B) 在醫院
(C) 在健身中心
(D) 在學校

- camp
  n. 營地，營區

93

What must be signed?

什麼一定要簽署？

正解 **(C)**

(A) A sales contract
(B) A sign-in sheet
(C) A health form
(D) A file

(A) 銷售合約
(B) 簽到表
(C) 健康報告表
(D) 檔案文件

- contract
  n. 合約
- sign-in sheet
  簽到表
- file
  n. 文件，檔案

94

What will be the last activity?

最後一項活動為何？

正解 **(A)**

(A) A tour of the weight room
(B) Questions will be
    answered
(C) A medical checkup
(D) An outdoor party

(A) 參觀舉重室
(B) 回答問題
(C) 健康檢查
(D) 戶外派對

- activity
  n. 活動
- checkup
  n. (健康)檢查
- outdoor
  a. 戶外的

Questions 95 through 97 refer to the following information.

Good morning and welcome to the Bellage Hotel. Please take advantage of our complimentary continental breakfast served from 6:00 to 10:00 every morning in the patio. In the afternoons, we have tea and coffee free for all guests. And in the evening in our atrium, we feature hors d'oeuvres and drinks, also complimentary from 6:00 to 11:00. For your convenience, we offer a shuttle service to nearby shopping malls and the convention center. And for a small fee, the shuttle service is also available for trips to nearby tourist spots. For details and / or reservations, please contact the front desk. Again, thank you for staying at the Bellage Hotel. Please let us know if we can be of any service.

請參考以下的資訊：

　　　各位早安！歡迎光臨 Bellage 飯店。請盡情享用我們在露台供應的免費歐陸早餐，時間從每天早上六點到十點。下午，我們免費提供給所有賓客茶和咖啡。傍晚，在中庭特別介紹開胃小菜和各類飲料，從六點到十一點也是免費供應的。同時為了方便各位，我們提供接駁車到附近的商場和會議中心。另外前往附近景點亦有接駁服務，費用低廉。欲知詳情或作預約，請洽詢櫃檯。再次感謝您光臨 Bellage 飯店。有任何需要服務的地方，請隨時告知我們。

Word Bank

• take advantage of	利用…	• complimentary	*a.* 免費贈送的
• continental breakfast	歐陸早餐	• patio	*n.* 露台，平台
• guest	*n.* 客人，賓客	• atrium	*n.* 庭院，中庭
• feature	*v.* 特別介紹(廣告)	• hors d'oeuvres	開胃小菜(法文)
• convenience	*n.* 方便，便利	• shuttle	*n.* 穿梭運輸，往返接送
• convention	*n.* 會議	• available	*a.* 可獲得的，可用的
• tourist spot	景點	• detail	*n.* 細節，詳情

中　文　翻　譯　和　解　答

95

Where are hors d'oeuvres served?　開胃小菜在哪裡提供？　**正解** **(C)**

(A) In the patio
(B) In the lobby
(C) In the atrium
(D) In your room

(A) 在庭院
(B) 在大廳
(C) 在中庭
(D) 在你的房間

· lobby *n.* 大廳

96

What service requires a fee?　何種服務需要付費？　**正解** **(C)**

(A) Breakfast
(B) Tea and coffee
(C) Transportation to tour sites
(D) Drinks

(A) 早餐
(B) 茶和咖啡
(C) 接駁車服務
(D) 傳真服務

· shuttle
  n. 往返運送

97

What time does the breakfast end?　早餐供應到幾點？　**正解** **(A)**

(A) 10:00 a.m.
(B) 11:00 a.m.
(C) 4:00 p.m.
(D) It's available all day.

(A) 早上十點
(B) 早上十一點
(C) 下午四點
(D) 全天供應

· available
  a. 可獲得的

Questions 98 through 100 refer to the following information.

Wiring money overseas is not a difficult thing. In fact, it can be quite easy if we have the correct information. First, we will need the bank's name, branch, address, telephone number and bank code. We also need the recipient's account name and number. And finally, we will need your signature on the wire registration form. After all of these have been completed, you will be able to request a wire transfer of funds via our 24-hour customer service line.

請參考以下的訊息：

匯錢到國外一點都不難。實際上，只要有正確資訊就相當簡單。首先，我們需要銀行行名、分行名稱、地址、電話和行庫代號。我們也需要收款人的戶名和帳號。最後我們還需要你在匯款單上簽名。完成這些程序後，您就能透過我們24小時的服務專線申請匯款。

Word Bank

• wire	*v.* 電匯	• overseas	*a./adv.* 向海外(的)
• in fact	事實上	• branch	*n.* 分公司，分行
• bank code	銀行代號	• recipient	*n.* 接受者，收受者
• signature	*n.* 簽名	• wire registration form	電匯單
• registration	*n.* 登記，註冊	• wire transfer	電匯，電子轉帳
• request	*v.* 要求，請求	• fund	*n.* 基金，專款，金錢
• via	*prep.* 透過，通過		

中　文　翻　譯　和　解　答

98

What is being discussed?

(A) Opening a bank account
(B) Applying for a credit card
(C) Sending money
(D) Finding a good bank

這是在談論什麼事？

(A) 銀行開戶
(B) 申請信用卡
(C) 寄錢
(D) 尋找好銀行

正解 **(C)**

・apply
　v. 申請

99

What is needed for this process?

(A) A deposit
(B) A big bank account
(C) A signature
(D) An e-mail address

手續上有何要求？

(A) 押金
(B) 銀行大戶
(C) 簽名
(D) 電子信箱地址

正解 **(C)**

・process
　n. 過程
・deposit
　n. 訂(押)金，
　　保證金，存款

100

What is an advantage of this?

(A) You can do it by phone.
(B) You can get a gift.
(C) You can go overseas.
(D) You don't have to sign anything.

這個程序有何優點？

(A) 你可以透過電話操作。
(B) 你可以得到禮品。
(C) 你可以到國外去。
(D) 你不需要簽字。

正解 **(A)**

・advantage
　n. 優點，優勢
・overseas
　adv. 在海外，
　　在國外

Part 5

101

Ms. Max is going to take a trip to Paris with her fiancé ------- her holiday.

(A) on
(B) during
(C) in
(D) while

休假期間，Max小姐將和未婚夫一起去巴黎度假。

(A) 在…
(B) 在…期間
(C) 在…方面
(D) 當…的時候

正解 **(A)** on

- fiancé　　　　*n.* 未婚夫，fiancée 未婚妻
- on one's holiday　在休假

102

They say Mr. Rose has ------- to do with the bankruptcy of Signtech because he was in another company when it happened.

(A) everything
(B) anything
(C) nothing
(D) something

他們說Rose先生和Signtech公司的倒閉沒有任何關係，因為當事情發生時，他在另一家公司。

(A) 每件事
(B) 無論何事
(C) 無關
(D) 某事

正解 **(C)** nothing

- bankruptcy *n.* 破產，倒閉

103

The latest upgraded model ------- the value of Songtech Company, so the company expects to increase its profit.

(A) deflects
(B) causes
(C) accredits
(D) enhances

新近升級的產品提升了Songtech公司的價值，因此預期該公司的收益會增加。

(A) 轉移
(B) 導致
(C) 確認…有資格
(D) 提高

正解 **(D)** enhances ; enhance 提高

- upgrade *v.* 提升，提高

中　文　翻　譯　和　解　答

104

As Carol made repeated mistakes on her night-duty, she was ------- yesterday.

(A) negotiated
(B) duplicated
(C) separated
(D) terminated

因為Carol值夜班時再三犯錯，她昨天被解雇了。

(A) 協商，談判
(B) 複製
(C) 隔開，分開
(D) 免職，解雇

正解 **(D)** terminated ; terminate 免職，解雇

・night-duty *n.* 值夜班

105

The customer service center has received a lot more complaints than expected as ------- May 15.

(A) of
(B) by
(C) since
(D) on

自五月十五日以來，客服中心已經受理了比預期要多的投訴。

(A) of
(B) by
(C) since
(D) on

正解 **(A)** of ; as of / from 從…以來

・complaint *n.* 投訴，申訴

106

The movie theater was ------- with audience on the evening of the fatal fire disaster.

(A) crowd
(B) crowded
(C) crowding
(D) crowds

致命的火災發生當晚，電影院擠滿了觀眾。

(A) 人群
(B) 擠滿
(C) 擠著
(D) 群眾

正解 **(B)** crowded ; crowd 擠滿

・fatal *a.* 致命的　　　　・disaster *n.* 災難

107

It's best to optimize your press ------- so they can be readily searched and browsed.

(A) news
(B) messages
(C) releases
(D) coverage

最好盡可能使你的新聞稿內容完善，這樣就易於被搜尋和瀏覽。

(A) 新聞，消息
(B) 消息，音訊
(C) 發佈的新聞(消息)
(D) 新聞報導

正解 **(C)** releases 發佈的新聞(消息)

· optimize *v.* 最優化，有效化　　· browse *v.* 瀏覽

108

After going on a hike, Warren realized that he couldn't walk as fast as a few years ago when he was in -------.

(A) cosy
(B) good
(C) perfect
(D) shape

Warren在徒步旅行後，瞭解自己已無法像兩三年前健康良好時一樣，走得那麼快。

(A) 溫暖舒適的
(B) 好的
(C) 完美的
(D) 健康狀況

正解 **(D)** shape；in shape 健康良好，體格健壯

· hike *n.* 徒步旅行，遠足 → go on (for) a hike 作徒步旅行

109

Relatively few people ever stop and decide what their top ------- is and work on that first.

(A) priority
(B) priorize
(C) prior
(D) priorties

相對而言，很少人會停下來，選擇最重要的事，然後優先努力去做。

(A) 重點(名詞)
(B) 確定優先順序(動詞)
(C) 先前的(形容詞)
(D) 重點(複數)

正解 **(A)** priority；此處為名詞形

· relatively *adv.* 相對而言　　· priority *n.* 優先考慮的事

中　文　翻　譯　和　解　答

110

If one wants to ------- a good impression at a job interview, it is best not to smoke or chatter.

如果在工作面試時，要讓對方留下好印象的話，最好不要吸煙或喋喋不休。

(A) have
(B) make
(C) keep
(D) get

(A) 有
(B) 留下
(C) 保持
(D) 得到

正解 **(B)** make或leave亦可

- impression　**n.** 印象
- chatter　　**v.** 喋喋不休
- interview　**n.** 面談(試)

111

Our company ------- all employees to wear identification badges when we enter our plant.

公司要求所有員工，在進入工廠時要佩戴識別證。

(A) slects
(B) requires
(C) admits
(D) concedes

(A) 選擇
(B) 要求
(C) 允許
(D) 承認

正解 **(B)** requires

戴識別證是規定，故公司可以要求或命令。

- identification　**n.** 識別；身份證明
- badge　**n.** 證章
- require　　　**v.** 要求；命令

112

The express train ------- at the terminal half hour ago.

特快車在半個小時前抵達總站。

(A) arrived
(B) has arrived
(C) had arrived
(D) is arrived

(A) 到達
(B) 已到達
(C) 曾到達
(D) 被到達

正解 **(A)** arrived

ago以前，既是提到過去的事情，自然要用過去式arrived。

- terminal　**n.** 總站；乘客集散站；(電腦)終端機

中 文 翻 譯 和 解 答

113

The whole workforce felt justified to take strike action because they complained ------- about working conditions.

(A) unlikey
(B) bitterly
(C) carelessly
(D) terribly

全體勞工認為採取罷工行動是對的,因為他們對工作條件相當不滿。

(A) 不太可能
(B) 憤恨地
(C) 不小心地
(D) 非常地

正解 **(B)** bitterly

　　bitterly是「憤憤不平地」,符合句意,是正答。

・workforce ***n.*** 勞工,全體從業人員 　・justify ***v.*** 證明…正確
・terribly ***adv.*** 非常,極

114

Professor Wu, ------- born in Taiwan, lived and practiced law in Hong Kong.

(A) even
(B) he was
(C) although
(D) who he was

吳教授雖然出生在台灣,但是住在香港開業當律師。

(A) 即使
(B) 他是
(C) 雖然
(D) 他是

正解 **(C)** although

　　答案(C)是 although he was 的省略,although born in Taiwan 是分詞構句的寫法。although是連接詞,有連結前後句的功能。

・practice ***v.*** 執業,開業

115

She asked me whether Smith had the capability -------.

(A) doing that
(B) to do that
(C) do that
(D) of doing that

她問我是否Smith有能力作那件事。

(A) doing that
(B) to do that
(C) do that
(D) of doing that

正解 **(B)** to do that

　　have the capability to do ~ 有能力做…,也可用 be capable of doing ~。

・capability ***n.*** 能力,才能

184

中　文　翻　譯　和　解　答

116

In spite of his proposal, the president agreed to consider ------- a raise in salary.

(A) to request
(B) request
(C) requesting
(D) requested

無視於他的建議，總經理依然同意考慮加薪的要求。

(A) 要求(不定詞)
(B) 要求(原形動詞)
(C) 要求(現在分詞)
(D) 要求(過去分詞)

正解 **(C)** requesting
consider的後面，要用**動名詞**作它的受詞。

・ in spite of = despite 不顧　　・ request　v. 要求，請求

117

All exhibitors ------- their displays since last Friday for the upcoming international trade exhibition.

(A) have prepared
(B) will prepare
(C) prepare
(D) prepared

所有參展廠商為了即將到來的國際貿易展，從上週五就開始準備他們的參展品。

(A) have prepared
(B) will prepare
(C) prepare
(D) prepared

正解 **(A)** have prepared；since和現在完成式一起使用。
・ exhibitor　n. 參展者　　・ display　n. 展覽(品)，陳列(品)
・ upcoming　a. 即將來臨的　・ exhibition　n. 展覽(會)

118

Ms. Thompson is ------- with her money because she wants to buy a gorgeous car.

(A) economic
(B) economical
(C) economized
(D) economically

Thompson小姐用錢很節儉，因為她要買一部漂亮的車子。

(A) 經濟的
(B) 節儉的
(C) 削減
(D) 節儉地

正解 **(B)** economical 節儉的

・ gorgeous　a. 非常漂亮的，極好的

119

Mr. Douglas always ------- assured that we will be successful on any project he assigns us.

(A) rests
(B) makes
(C) sees
(D) has

Douglas先生總是很有把握，我們將會圓滿完成他交付的任何計劃。

(A) 放在，停留
(B) 做成
(C) 看到
(D) 已經

正解　**(A)** rests；rest assured 肯定，感到有把握

· assign　*v.* 指派，交付

120

More than half of the executives firmly believed the president in his financial ------- plan.

(A) resrore
(B) restoration
(C) restored
(D) restorative

半數以上的高層主管堅信總經理在財務重整方面的計劃。

(A) resrore
(B) restoration
(C) restored
(D) restorative

正解　**(B)** restoration；*n.*＋*n.* 前面的 *n.* 可作 *a.* 修飾後面的 *n.*

· executives　*n.* 高層主管　　· restoration　*n.* 修復，恢復

121

The smart marketers of today create compelling messages and tell prospective customers directly ------- Web-powered communication tools.

(A) use
(B) uses
(C) using
(D) used

現在聰明的行銷人創造出扣人心弦的訊息，並且運用網路溝通工具，直接訴諸可能的顧客。

(A) use
(B) uses
(C) using
(D) used

正解　**(C)** using

· compelling　*a.* 引人入勝的，有強烈吸引力的

中　文　翻　譯　和　解　答

122

We still wonder who will make a business ------- to Singapore to negotiate with Northwest Technology.

(A) travel
(B) tour
(C) trip
(D) journey

我們還不知道誰會到新加坡出差，去和西北科技公司談判。

(A) 旅行
(B) 旅遊，遊覽
(C) 旅行
(D) 長途旅程

正解 **(C)** trip 旅行

・business trip 出差　　　　　・negotiate　**v.** 協商，談判

123

Lifetech company is privately held and does not disclose -------, but it is clear this is a growing business.

(A) perks
(B) savings
(C) income
(D) revenues

Lifetech公司是私人企業，沒有公開營業收入，但是很顯然這是一家成長中的企業。

(A) 津貼，額外收入
(B) 存款
(C) 所得，收入
(D) 營收，收入

正解 **(D)** revenues 營收，收入

・privately　**adv.** 私有地，私自地　　・disclose　**v.** 公開，透露

124

Before being traded to the Panthers, he ------- the greatest relief pitcher in the long history of the Eagles.

(A) had been
(B) is
(C) has been
(D) will be

在被交換到美洲豹隊之前，他一直是老鷹隊最棒的後援投手。

(A) had been
(B) is
(C) has been
(D) will be

正解 **(A)** had been。 being traded 是 he was traded 的省略，before 的子句用過去式，主要子句自然要用表示「過去之前的過去」的過去完成式。

・trade　**v.** 用…交換，交易，做生意　・relief **n.** 後援者，接替者，換班者
・pitcher　**n.** 投手

125

Wanda and Harvey ------- to Hawaii next fall even though it is a very busy time for them.

(A) are coming
(B) aren't coming
(C) have come
(D) came

雖然對 Wanda 和 Harvey 來說，明年秋天他們會很忙，但他們還是會到Hawaii來。

(A) 將來到
(B) 不會來
(C) 已來到
(D) 來過

正解 **(A)** are coming
　　　next fall 明年秋天，要用未來時態，(A)是正答。

　・even though　雖然，儘管

126

You should not criticize someone until you --------in his shoes.

(A) talk a while
(B) walk a mile
(C) work all day
(D) work a while

你沒了解別人的立場前，不應該批評人。

(A) 談一陣子
(B) 走一哩路
(C) 整天工作
(D) 工作一陣子

正解 **(B)** walk a mile
　　　walk a mile in someone's shoes 了解某人的立場（處境），符合句意。

　・criticize *v.* 批評，指責

127

He thought the sales meeting was on Thursday or Friday so imagine his surprise when he found out it was going to ------- on Saturday.

(A) be held
(B) have held
(C) hold
(D) hold on

他原以為業務會議是在週四或週五，所以可以想見當他發現會議是在週六舉行時，他會多麼驚訝。

(A) 被舉行
(B) 已舉行
(C) 舉行
(D) 等著

正解 **(A)** be held。會議是「被」舉行、「被」召開，所以要用被動態。

　・sales meeting　業務會議　　・imagine　*v.* 想像
　・surprise　*n.* 驚訝，吃驚　　・find out　發現，查明

中 文 翻 譯 和 解 答

128

They are on the company's expense account and can run ------- the bill as high as they like.

(A) down
(B) out
(C) over
(D) up

他們是由公司支付費用，而且可以隨心所欲花用。

(A) 衰退
(B) 耗盡
(C) 撞倒輾過
(D) 提高

正解 **(D)** up。run up the bill 是「提高金額」的意思，符合句意，故(D) 是正答。run down 則是「減小，衰退」，run out 是「結束，耗盡」，run over 是「撞倒且輾過」，都不符句意。

・expense account 交際費，出差支出帳目

129

Las Vegas has many conventions and is very crowded at that time of year so you should ------- a hotel room well in advance of your visit.

(A) book
(B) call
(C) make
(D) reservation

拉斯維加斯有許多會議，而且每年那時候都非常擁擠，所以你應該在造訪之前，先預訂好旅館房間。

(A) 預約
(B) 呼叫
(C) 製造
(D) 預訂 (*n.*)

正解 **(A)** book
・助動詞 should 後面接**原形動詞**，依句意「預約旅館房間」，應該用 book a hotel room， 故(A)是正答。

・convention　　*n.* 會議，大會　　・crowded　　　*a.* 擁擠的
・book　　　　　*v.* 預約，約定　　・in advance of　　在…之前（先）

130

The sales department has spent over a month working on this proposal so if they get turned ------- they will be very disappointed.

業務部門已經花了一個多月進行這項計劃，所以如果他們遭到拒絕，他們將會非常失望。

(A) down
(B) in
(C) over
(D) up

(A) turn down 拒絕
(B) turn in 交出
(C) turn over 把…移交
(D) turn up 使增加速度

正解 **(A)** down。turn down 拒絕，符合句意，(A)是正答。

・turn in 獲得，產生，交出　　・turn over 把…移交，仔細考慮
・turn up 使增加速度（力量）

131

It is a long application but you only have to ------- in the boxes that are marked to save you some time.

它是一份很長的申請書，但為了節省你一些時間，你只需填妥作了記號的框格。

(A) call
(B) sign
(C) drop
(D) fill

(A) call in 收回
(B) sign in 簽到
(C) drop in 順便過來
(D) fill in 填寫

正解 **(D)** fill。fill in 填寫，符合句意，是正答。

・application　*n.* 申請書，申請　　・box　　*n.* 框格
・call in　　　　拜訪，收回　　　　・sign in　　簽到
・drop in　　　　順便過來

中　文　翻　譯　和　解　答

132

Because she was such a generous and caring person, many people ------- kindly of her at her retirement party.

(A) gave
(B) said
(C) spoke
(D) took

因為她是非常慷慨又有愛心的人,許多人都在她的退休宴會上,說了她很多好話。

(A) 給
(B) 說
(C) 說
(D) 取

正解 **(C)** spoke。speak kindly of ～ 說…好話,符合句意,是正答。

　・generous　　*a.* 慷慨的,大方的　　・caring　　*a.* 關心別人的,有愛心的
　・retirement　　*n.* 退休

133

Right now we are doing well because we were able to anticipate the downturn in the economy while the other companies ------- like the boom would last forever.

(A) acted
(B) have acted
(C) will acted
(D) act

現在我們的生意很好,因為當其它公司還依照繁榮長久持續時期的作法,我們早已預期到經濟的衰退。

(A) acted
(B) have acted
(C) will acted
(D) act

正解 **(A)** acted

　・downturn　　*n.* 衰退,降低,蕭條　　・boom　　　　*n.* 繁榮,景氣,繁榮時期
　・last　　　　*v.* 持續,延續,持久　　・compensate　*v.* 賠償,補償
　・concentrate　*v.* 集中,專心,注意　　・reject　　　　*v.* 拒絕,丟棄

134

With the low morale of the office and the sad state of the economy, there is ------- we would ever take on another project right now.

(A) another way
(B) a way
(C) no way
(D) some way

辦公室的士氣低迷，再加上經濟不佳的情況，此刻我們可能無法再承接其它的企劃案。

(A) 另一方法
(B) 一個方法
(C) 沒有辦法
(D) 有些方法

正解 **(C)** no way 沒有方法（辦法），無法；符合句意，故(C)是正答。
 ・morale *n.* 士氣，鬥志　　 ・sad state 糟糕的情況

135

This meeting may have to take longer than we expected if we are going to ------- at an agreement we can all live with.

(A) arrive
(B) get
(C) laugh
(D) look

如果我們要達成大家都能接受的協議，會議可能必須花比預期還要長的時間。

(A) 達成
(B) 拿到
(C) 笑
(D) 看

正解 **(A)** arrive。arrive at 有「達成，作出」之意，符合句意，故(A)是正答。
 ・agreement *n.* 協議，意見一致　 ・live with 容忍，忍受

136

The forest fires burned for three days until the soldiers and firefighters were able to get the situation ------- .

(A) prohibited
(B) out of control
(C) safe
(D) under control

這場森林大火燃燒了三天，一直到軍人與消防隊員能夠將情況控制住。

(A) 禁止的
(B) 失去控制
(C) 安全的
(D) 得到控制，在控制中

正解 **(D)** under control
get the situation under control 讓情況得到控制，符合句意，故(D)是正答。

 ・firefighter *n.* 消防人員，救火員　 ・flame *n.* 火焰，火舌

中　文　翻　譯　和　解　答

137

According to the news, there were ------- 100 people trapped in the building at the time of the fire.

(A) estimated
(B) an estimated
(C) the estimating
(D) estimation

根據新聞報導，火災當時估計有100個人受困在大樓裡。

(A) estimated
(B) an estimated
(C) the estimating
(D) estimation

正解　**(B)** an estimated

an estimated 本應為 an estimated amount of，通常可將 amount of 省略。

- according to ~　根據…，依照…　　• estimate　*v.* 估計，評估
- trap　　　　　*v.* 困住，攔住，關住

138

Raymond could barely ------- his smile at the thought of how much money he was going to make.

(A) contain
(B) envelop
(C) maintain
(D) include

Raymond一想到自己會賺多少錢，就忍不住想笑。

(A) 抑制
(B) 裹住
(C) 維持
(D) 包含

正解　**(A)** contain

contain有「抑制、控制、克制」的意思；envelop「把…包住、裹住」，maintain「維持、保持」，include「包含、包括」。顯然用 contain his smile 比較適合。

- barely　　　*adv.* 幾乎沒有，僅僅　• at the thought of ~　一想到…
- make money　　賺錢，掙錢

139

The customer's visits to the plant are too ------- for the manager to get acquainted with her.

(A) unfamiliar
(B) efficient
(C) definite
(D) infrequent

這個客戶很少來到工廠，所以經理不認識她。

(A) 不了解的
(B) 有效率的
(C) 明確的
(D) 不常的

正解 **(D)** infrequent

字首 **in-** 是 not 之意，infrequent「不常的、罕有的」。(D) 符合題意，才是正答。

• plant　　　*n.* 工廠　　　• get (be) acquainted with ~ 和…互相認識
• unfamiliar　*a.* 不了解的　• definite　*a.* 明確的

140

Every month we keep getting more and more instructions, and they are getting too hard to keep ------- with.

(A) ahead
(B) down
(C) forward
(D) up

每個月我們都不斷地收到更多的指示，同時也愈來愈難趕上進度。

(A) ahead
(B) down
(C) forward
(D) up

正解 **(D)** up

keep up with 是「跟上，趕上」的意思，符合句意，(D)是正答。

• instruction　*n.* 指示

NO MATERIAL ON THIS PAGE

Part 6

Questions 141-143 refer to the following message.

Which is more valuable? To provide a $60,000 heart transplant for an _____ child of indigent parents? Or to use that money

141. (A) ail
(B) ailed
(C) ailing
(D) ailment

for prenatal care that may enhance the life expectancy of fetuses being carried by 100 expectant mothers? Surely the leaders of the democratic capitalist world can afford both. _____ a growing

142. (A) Although
(B) Yet
(C) When
(D) Then

number of health experts argue that most developed countries, in fact, no longer has the financial resources to provide _____

143. (A) unlimited
(B) infinite
(C) exclusive
(D) profitable

medical treatment for all those who need it. The only solution, they say, is rationing health care.

中譯

　　哪一種較有價值？為貧窮父母的生病小孩，提供六萬美元的心臟移植手術？或者把同樣的金錢花在產前照顧，而可能提高一百位孕婦對胎兒生命的期待？當然，民主的資本主義世界的領導者，有能力負擔以上這兩者。但是，愈來愈多的醫療保健專家認為：事實上，大多數已開發國家不再有財力，提供給所有需要的人無限制的醫療照顧。他們表示，唯一的解決之道，就是定額分配的醫療保健。

解答

141 **(C)** ailing

142 **(B)** yet

143 **(A)** unlimited

Word Bank

· valuable	*a.* 有價值的，有用的	· transplant	*n.* 移植
· ailing	*a.* 生命的	· indigent	*a.* 貧窮的
· prenatal	*a.* 產前的	· expectancy	*n.* 期待，期望
· fetus = foetus	*n.* 胎兒	· expectant	*a.* 即將生孩子的
· capitalist	*n.* 資本家	· afford	*v.* 能堪，提供，付得起
· unlimited	*a.* 無限制的	· infinite	*a.* 無限的
· exclusive	*a.* 獨有的，獨享的	· profitable	*a.* 有利可圖的
· treatment	*n.* 治療，待遇	· appropriate	*a.* 適當的
· solution	*n.* 解決(方法)	· rationing	*a.* 定量分配的

Questions 144-146 refer to the following article.

Everybody wants to look healthy and feel energetic. Getting in shape requires exercise. Some people make their decisions to get back into shape with a _____ to the mall to buy

144. (A) trip
(B) travel
(C) sightseeing
(D) glance

exercise outfits and equipment that can cost hundreds of dollars while others spend a lot of money on fitness center memberships. What a senseless waste it is!

_____ , if you do make the decision to start

145. (A) Supposedly
(B) Therefore
(C) Likewise
(D) Otherwise

exercising, start slowly. If you jog, you can find a good pair of running shoes for 60-70 dollars. If you join a health club, try a _____ membership. Before you make that big purchase

146. (A) tried
(B) try
(C) trial
(D) trying

for fitness, make sure you have the willpower to get in shape first.

中　譯

　　每個人都想要看起來健康,同時感覺很有活力。想練好身體就需要運動。有些人決定保持健美,就走一趟購物商場,去購買價值數百美金的全套運動服裝和器材,而其他人則花許多錢成為健身中心的會員。這真是無謂的浪費!

　　因此,如果你真的下決心要開始運動,就慢慢地開始。如果要慢跑,你可以找一雙60到70塊美金、好的跑步鞋。如果要加入健身俱樂部,不妨先參加體驗會員。在你為了健身而大肆採購之前,首先要確定你真的有保持健身的意志力!

解　答

144	(A) trip	**146**	(C) trial
145	(B) Therefore		

Word Bank

· energetic	*a.* 充滿活力的		· fitness	*n.* 身體健康,體能
· get in (into) shape	練好身體		· outfit	*n.* 全套服裝
· membership	*n.* 會員(身份)		· jog	*v.* 慢跑

Questions 147-149 refer to the following article.

$\mathbb{H}$aving been made possible by improvements in international shipping, now it is easier to send computer parts and raw materials nearly anywhere today _____ a much less expensive

147. (A) at
    (B) in
    (C) on
    (D) with

price than 20 years ago. However, one change of the technology has meant a steep rise in production costs for every computermaker. Consumers are demanding a higher rate of perfection today. At present, a problem with production can also mean a class action, but years ago it would only have necessitated a _____.

148. (A) withdrawal
    (B) protection
    (C) recall
    (D) termination

Therefore new and expensive technologies have _____ to

149. (A) come
    (B) gone
    (C) turned
    (D) gotten

be used to minimize the possibility of making defective computers.

　　跨國運輸的進步，使得現在更容易運送電腦零件和原料到各地，而且費用比二十年前更低。然而，對每個電腦廠商來說，一項技術的改變，就意味著一次生產成本的劇增。現在消費者要求更完美的品質。數年前，生產過程的瑕疵，可能只要回收產品就能解決；今天，這問題卻可能意味著集體訴訟。因此，新而昂貴的技術，結果是用來減少製造有瑕疵電腦的可能性。

解　　答

| 147 | **(A)** at | 149 | **(A)** come |
| 148 | **(C)** recall | | |

Word Bank

· raw	*a.* 生的，原始的	· steep	*a.* 急遽的
· demand	*v.* 要求	· rate	*n.* 比率
· perfection	*n.* 完美	· class action	集體訴訟
· necessitate	*v.* 使成為必要	· minimize	*v.* 使…減到最低
· protection	*n.* 防護物	· withdrawal	*n.* 取消，提款
· recall	*n.* 回收(不良產品)	· termination	*n.* 終止，結束

Questions 150-152 refer to the following letter.

Dear Friend,

　　The Anti-Pollution Committee of the Super Sugar Refinery is pleased to inform you that an anti-pollution program will be started for nearby residents next month.

　　It is our aim to win the residents' support of this district to fight pollution. Due to the fact that you have recently moved _____ the newly-completed estate of Grand Building, it is

150. (A) around
(B) on
(C) into
(D) up

with much pleasure that our Committee is going to provide service to you as well.

　　To publicize the work of our Committee, an anti-pollution program _____ especially for the residents of Grand

151. (A) erupted
(B) held
(C) ended
(D) concluded

Building includes a press conference and door-to-door visits. The press conference will be held on Saturday morning (May 25). As for the visits which will mainly be _____ in the

152. (A) selected
(B) engaged
(C) erected
(D) conducted

evening between 8 p.m. and 10 p.m. from Monday thru Thursday, our Committee would appreciate an opportunity to meet with you to explain our services in detail.

　　If there are any questions, please call our free number, 0800-123-123.

Yours faithfully,

Smith Wang

Smith Wang
Chairman,
Anti-Pollution Committee of Super Sugar Refinery

親愛的朋友，

　　超級糖廠反污染委員會很樂意通知您，下個月我們將為附近的芳鄰舉辦反污染活動。

　　我們的目標是：贏得本地區鄉親們的支持，來對抗污染。您最近已遷入新建完工的Grand大廈社區，我們委員會也相當樂意為您服務。

　　為了宣揚我們委員會的工作，我們特別為Grand大廈社區居民，舉辦一個反污染活動，包括記者會以及挨家挨戶的拜訪。記者會將在週六早上(五月二十五日)舉行。至於拜訪，將於週一至週四的晚間八時至十時進行，我們委員會很重視能和您見面的機會，以便向您詳細說明我們的服務內容。

　　如有任何疑問，請立刻撥打免付費電話0800-123-123。

超級糖廠反污染委員會主委

Smith Wang　敬上

150 (C) into

151 (B) held

152 (D) conducted

Word Bank

· anti-pollution	*n.* 反污染	· refinery	*n.* 精煉廠，提煉廠
· resident	*n.* 居民，定居者	· district	*n.* 地區
· estate	*n.* 住宅區；財產	· publicize	*v.* 公佈；宣揚
· erupt	*v.* 爆發	· press conference	記者會
· door-to-door	*a.* 挨家挨戶的，逐戶的	· select	*v.* 選擇
· engage	*v.* 吸引；聘用	· erect	*v.* 豎立；建立
· conduct	*v.* 進行；引導	· detail	*n.* 詳情；細節

Part 7

Questions 153-154 refer to the following letter.

HSC Motors Company, Inc.
1234 Juarez Ave.,
Hermosa, CA 87342

Dear New Car Owner,

Thank you for your recent purchase of a 2008 HSC sports utility vehicle.

Customer safety and satisfaction is the number one concern for us here at HSC Motors. Therefore, we are contacting all owners of the 2008 CoSpeed TEC to alert them to a potential malfunction in the brake light electrical system of this model. It has come to our attention that in some instances, the brake lights fail to turn off when the brake pedal is no longer depressed.

Our electrical engineers have developed a simple and easy-to-install device for this problem. It would be our pleasure to have this installed for you at no cost. In order to make this as convenient as possible for you, your nearest HSC Motors dealers will dispatch a mechanic to your home or work, at no extra charge. Installations may also be done at your dealership. Simply call the dealership where your CoSpeed was purchased to set up an appointment. We truly apologize for any inconvenience.

Sincerely,

Juan Howard

Executive Vice-President,
Sales Development

問題 **153-154** 請參考以下的信件。

HSC汽車公司
加州Hermosa市Juarez大道1234號
郵遞區號87342

親愛的新車主，

　　感謝您最近購買一輛2008型的HSC多功能跑車。
　　顧客的安全與滿意是我們HSC汽車公司最重要的考量。因此我們特別提醒所有2008型CoSpeed TEC的車主注意，請對此款車型可能發生故障的煞車燈電子系統提高警覺。我們已經注意到在某些情況下，當煞車踏板不能減壓時，煞車燈無法自動關閉。
　　我們的電子工程師已經針對這項問題，研發了一種簡便安裝的裝置。我們很樂意免費地為您安裝。為了您的方便，距離您最近的HSC汽車經銷商，將派遣修理技師免費到您府上或辦公地點服務。您也可以在經銷商所在地進行安裝。只要打電話給當時購買CoSpeed TEC汽車的經銷商，安排預約時間即可。造成您的不便，我們深感抱歉。

衷心地祝福您！

業務部副總裁

Juan Howard

敬上

153

What is the purpose of this letter?

(A) To inform engineers of a design flaw.
(B) To advertise a new car model.
(C) To recommend tips on driver safety.
(D) To announce a parts replacement.

這封信的目的為何? **正解 (D)**

(A) 通知工程師有關設計上的缺陷。
(B) 為新款的車打廣告。
(C) 建議安全駕駛技巧。
(D) 公佈有關零件的更換。

154

Why would customers call their dealership?

(A) To get someone to come over and fix the problem.
(B) To complain about the services.
(C) To talk to an engineer about the brake pedal.
(D) To purchase a new CoSpeed at a discount.

為何客戶要打電話給他們的經銷商? **正解 (A)**

(A) 找人過來解決問題。
(B) 抱怨服務不佳。
(C) 和技師談論煞車踏板。
(D) 以折扣價購買新的CoSpeed汽車。

Word Bank

• purchase	*n./v.*	購買(物)	• utility	*n.*	效用，實用的物品
• satisfaction	*n.*	滿意度	• concern	*n./v.*	關心(之事)
• alert	*v./n.*	(使)警覺	• malfunction	*n./v.*	故障
• brake light	*n.*	煞車燈	• attention	*n.*	注意力
• instance	*n.*	場合，情況	• pedal	*n.*	踏板
• depressed	*a.*	減壓的	• install	*v.*	安裝
• dispatch	*v.*	派遣	• mechanic	*n.*	修理工，技工
• installation	*n.*	安裝	• dealership	*n.*	代理/經銷權
• set up	*ph.*	建立	• device	*n.*	裝置，設備

Questions 155-157 refer to the following report.

A University of Denger poll of young people found some intriguing opinions about adulthood and maturity. Considering most kids start college at age 17 or 18, it's almost comical that the average age most expected to find a full-time job is 21.2. This either means a lot of kids take about three long years to find a full-time job after high school graduation or that college kids are skipping graduation ceremonies altogether and getting almost a year's head start in the job market. The poll did not break down the respondents according to education levels and has therefore left its findings open to a lot of criticism. Even so, the full results are fascinating:

Goal in life	Average age expected to achieve this goal
Self-support	20.9 years old
Moving out from parents' home	21.1 years old
First full-time job	21.2 years old
College graduation	22.3 years old
Financially able to support a family	24.5 years old
Married	25.7 years old
Birth of first child	26.2 years old

問題 **155-157** 請參考以下的報告。

　　一份Denger大學針對年輕人所做的調查發現，一些對於成年期和成長的有趣看法。大部分孩子在17或18歲開始上大學，他們多半期望能夠找到一份全職工作的平均年齡是21.2歲，這幾乎是很可笑的。這意味著很多孩子在高中畢業後，大約要花三年之久去找一份全職的工作，不然就是正在念大學的孩子，會跳過畢業典禮，幾乎提早一年就開始在職場工作。這份調查並未根據教育程度對受訪者做區分，也因此讓調查結果遭到很多批評。即便如此，這整個結果仍然是很有趣的。

人生的目標	預期完成該目標的平均年齡
自立	20.9 歲
搬離父母親的家	21.1 歲
第一份全職工作	21.2 歲
大學畢業	22.3 歲
財務自足養家	24.5 歲
結婚	25.7 歲
第一個小孩出生	26.2 歲

155

When do those polled think they should leave home?

(A) At 20.9 years of age.
(B) At 21.1 years of age.
(C) At 21.2 years of age.
(D) At 22.3 years of age.

那些受訪者認為他們應該何 **正解 (B)** 時離開家?

(A) 在20.9歲。
(B) 在21.1歲。
(C) 在21.2歲。
(D) 在22.3歲。

156

Why do some people criticize the results?

(A) The education level of the respondents is not given.
(B) The number of the respondents is too small.
(C) The questions are comical.
(D) Older people were not polled.

為何有些人批評這些結果? **正解 (A)**

(A) 未提供受訪者的教育程度。
(B) 受訪者的人數太少。
(C) 問題都太好笑。
(D) 未調查較年長的人。

157

How soon after college do the young people polled expect to be married?

(A) About 2 years.
(B) Within 3 years.
(C) About 3 and a half years.
(D) Four and a half years after.

受訪的年輕人希望在大學畢 **正解 (C)** 業之後多久結婚?

(A) 大約兩年。
(B) 三年以內。
(C) 大約三年半。
(D) 四年半之後。

Word Bank

· intriguing	*a.* 有趣的，引人入勝的	· opinion	*n.* 意見，看法
· adulthood	*n.* 成年期	· comical	*a.* 好笑的，滑稽的
· altogether	*adv.* 全部，全然	· respondent	*n.* 回答問題的人
· according to	*ph.* 根據	· criticism	*n.* 批評
· fascinating	*a.* 吸引人的，迷人的	· self-supporting	*a./n.* 自立(的)

Questions 158-159 refer to the following information.

※ *One-Hour Tours*
Across the waterfront. Departs at 12:00, 1:00, 2:00 and 3:00 from Point Hudson's Long Dock. Saturdays and Sundays only by this schedule. By charter weekdays. **$6**

※ *Two-Hour Tours*
Expanded waterfront tour, to view the waterfront, the Fort and Point Wilson areas. Depart and return at the Boat Haven Dock. Departs 12:30 weekdays only. **$12**

※ *Three-Hour Tours*
Leisurely ride to Sims Harbor, landing at Nordland's General Store as tides allow. By advanced reservation only. Departs 8:30 a.m. DAILY from Boat Haven Dock. **$20**

問題 **158-159** 請參考以下的資訊。

※ 一小時行程
橫越濱海地區。分別於12:00、1:00、2:00和3:00從Hudson岬角碼頭出發。本時間表僅適用於週六、週日，週一至週五則依規定開航。費用**6**元。

※ 兩小時行程
延伸的濱海之旅，遊覽Fort和Wilson岬角一帶的海域。在Haven碼頭上下船。只在週一至週五12:30出發。費用**12**元。

※ 三小時行程
Sims 港灣輕鬆遊，若潮汐狀況許可的話，會在Nordland大眾商店停靠。只接受事先預約。每天早上8:30從Haven碼頭出發。費用**20**元。

中　文　翻　譯　和　解　答

158

What is true about the information?

(A) The one-hour tours depart from Boat Haven Dock.
(B) The two-hour tours are scheduled only on weekdays.
(C) A three-hour tour costs twelve dollars.
(D) The leisurely rides land at Nordland's General Store daily.

以下的資訊何者為真？　　正解 **(B)**

(A) 一小時行程於Haven碼頭出發。
(B) 二小時行程僅於週間行駛。
(C) 三小時行程單趟費用12元。
(D) 輕鬆遊行程每天停靠Nordland大眾商店。

159

Which tour requires reservations?

(A) The two-hour tours.
(B) The three-hour tours.
(C) The expanded waterfront tours.
(D) They all require reservations.

何種行程需要預約？　　正解 **(B)**

(A) 兩小時行程。
(B) 三小時行程。
(C) 延伸的濱海行程。
(D) 都要預約。

Word Bank

- waterfront　　**n.** 港區，濱水地區
- point　　**n.** 岬角，尖岬
- expended　　**adj.** 展開的，擴大的
- leisurely　　**adv.** 悠閒地，從容不迫地
- schedule　　**v.** 排定時間表
- reservation　　**n.** 預訂，預約

- depart　　**v.** 出發，啟程
- charter　　**n.** 許可證，法令規定
- weekdays　　**n.** 工作日，週一至週五
- require　　**v.** 需要

Questions 160-162 refer to the following information.

● Orlando pledges 1% of sales to the preservation and restoration of the natural environment. For further information, please write to Orlando Environmental Program, Box 1019, Ventura, CA 94126.

● For a catalog, the name of your nearest dealer, or further information, call 1-800-530-9224 (U.S.A. and Canada only) or check out our Web site: www.orlando.com

● Please contact the store from which you bought your Orlando product for a refund, exchange or repair. For certain items, damage due to wear and tear will be repaired at a reasonable charge.

Care: Machine wash in cold water, gentle cycle. Line dry. Do not bleach.

問題 **160-162** 請參考以下的訊息。

● Orlando承諾將營業額的百分之一，用於自然環境的保護與重建。需要更多資料，請寫信到Orlando環境保護計劃 ——（郵遞區號94126）加州Ventura市，郵政1019號信箱。

● 需要索取目錄、附近的經銷商或更多資訊，請電1-800-530-9224（僅限美加地區），或上我們的網站查詢：www.orlando.com。

● 需要退換貨或修理，請向購貨商家洽詢。某些商品若因穿戴受損，需要修理，則酌收合理的費用。

注意事項：洗衣機洗滌請用冷水，低轉速，晾乾，請勿漂白！

中 文 翻 譯 和 解 答

160

What is NOT included in this information?

(A) How to wash the item.
(B) How to contact the company.
(C) How to get a catalog.
(D) How to reach the company by e-mail.

此資訊中未包括什麼內容？ 正解 **(D)**

(A) 如何清洗商品。
(B) 如何聯絡公司。
(C) 如何取得目錄。
(D) 如何以電子郵件聯絡公司。

161

What happens to 1% of the company's sales?

(A) It is given as bonuses to the management.
(B) It goes to the renovation of stores.
(C) It goes to charity.
(D) It is returned to the customers.

公司百分之一的銷售額會如 正解 **(C)**
何處理？

(A) 給管理階層作紅利金。
(B) 給店家整修用。
(C) 給慈善機關。
(D) 回饋顧客。

162

What best describes this company?

(A) Energy-efficient.
(B) Environmentally conscious.
(C) Cost-cutting.
(D) Anti-globalization.

什麼最能說明這家公司？ 正解 **(B)**

(A) 有效使用能源的。
(B) 有環保意識的。
(C) 削減成本的。
(D) 反全球化。

- pledge   *v.* 作保證，發誓
- restoration   *n.* 復原，修復，重建
- further   *a.* 進一步的，更多的，另加的
- program   *n.* 計劃，活動，節目
- dealer   *n.* 經銷商
- refund   *n.* 退還，退款
- certain   *a.* 某一個
- due to   由於
- reasonable   *a.* 合理的
- gentle cycle   輕微的轉速
- bleach   *v.* 漂白
- reach   *v.* 接觸，聯絡
- management   *n.* 管理階層
- charity   *n.* 慈善（機關），公益
- energy-efficient   *a.* 有效使用能源的
- cost-cutting   *a.* 削減成本的，削減費用的

- preservation   *n.* 保護，維護，保持
- environment   *n.* 環境
- information   *n.* 資料，資訊
- catalog   *n.* 目錄
- check out   查證，得到證實
- exchange   *n.* 交換，互換
- damage   *n.* 損壞，損失
- tear   *v.* 撕裂，撕壞
- charge   *n.* 收費
- line dry   晾乾
- include   *v.* 包括，包含
- bonus   *n.* 紅利，獎金
- renovation   *n.* 更新，革新，整修
- customer   *n.* 顧客，客戶
- conscious   *a.* 有意識的，有知覺的
- anti-globalization   *n.* 反全球化

Questions 163-166 refer to the following letter.

Dear Ms. Hartford,

If you watched the nightly news, by now you have heard the news of last night's fire that all but destroyed the Midwest Savings and Loan Association. As a depositor, no doubt this has raised your concern. But I am writing you as president of the institution to assure you that your savings is safe and we are well on the way to recovery.

It is true that the fire has completely destroyed our physical location. You will no longer be able to transact business at our Meadowland Road headquarters. But technology has enabled us to save the bulk of our operation, and your files and records are safe in our offsite storage facility. We will be ready to transact business within two days of your receiving this letter.

A temporary facility has been established at 2900 Broomsfield Court, where we will process over-the-counter transactions. If you have a checking account with us, your checks will continue to be accepted and processed through Greydon Trust, our correspondent bank. Your savings, insured by the Federal Deposit Insurance Corp., are available to you any time.

If you have any specific questions, feel free to call the Midwest hotline at 800-999-1234. We thank you for your patience. A disaster like this is never easy to overcome, but your support makes it that much easier.

Best regards,

Robert Hendricks

Robert Hendricks
President, Midwest Savings and Loan Association

問題 **163-166** 請參考以下的信件。

親愛的Hartford女士：

　　如果您看了晚間新聞，就已經知道昨晚的大火幾乎摧毀了Midwest儲蓄信用合作社。您是我們的存款戶，毫無疑問地，這會引起您的關心。我身為機構的總裁，以此信函向您保證您的存款安全無虞，而且我們也在順利復原中。

　　大火的確完全摧毀了我們的建築，您無法繼續在Meadowland路的總行進行交易，但科技讓我們能夠維持大部分的營運，同時您的檔案紀錄都好好地存放在另外的儲藏設施裡。您收到信後的兩天內，就可以進行交易。

　　我們已在Broomsfield Court 2900號設立臨時辦事處，可以進行櫃檯交易。倘若您有支票帳戶，您的支票可透過我們的聯行—Greydon信託—繼續使用。聯邦存款保險公司擔保您的存款，您可以隨時動用。

　　如果您有任何特別的問題，請隨時撥打800-999-1234 Midwest專線。感謝您的耐心包容。如此的災難雖然不易克服，但有了您的支持會更容易些，謝謝您！

　　　　　　　　　　　　　　　　　　Midwest儲蓄信用合作社總裁

　　　　　　　　　　　　　　　　　Robert Hendricks

　　　　　　　　　　　　　　　　　Robert Hendricks

　　　　　　　　　　　　　　　　　　　　　　　　　敬上

Word Bank

· nightly news		晚間新聞	· all but		幾乎，差不多
· destroy	*v.*	摧毀，毀壞	· depositor	*n.*	存款人，存戶
· concern	*n.*	關心，關懷	· recovery	*n.*	復原
· transact	*v.*	處理，辦理	· headquarters	*n.*	總部，總公司
· technology	*n.*	科技	· bulk	*n.*	大部份，大量
· file	*n.*	檔案	· storage	*n.*	儲存，保管，貯藏所
· facility	*n.*	設施	· temporary	*a.*	臨時的，暫時的
· establish	*v.*	設立，建立	· process	*v.*	進行
· correspondent	*a.*	一致的，符合的	· insure	*v.*	給…保險；保證，確保

163

Why was this letter sent?

(A) To let depositors know that fires at the bank are very unusual.
(B) To warn depositors of a fire at the bank.
(C) To ask depositors for help in rebuilding the bank.
(D) To assure depositors at the bank that their money is safe.

為何寄這封信？　　　**正解 (D)**

(A) 告知存戶銀行大火極不尋常。
(B) 警告存戶銀行失火。
(C) 要求存戶幫忙重建銀行。
(D) 保證銀行存戶的錢安全無虞。

164

What can depositors do until a permanent bank is established?

(A) Use the temporary bank.
(B) Wait a few days until the new bank is built.
(C) Open a checking account at Greydon Trust.
(D) Call the Federal Deposit Insurance Corp. to withdraw money.

在永久銀行建立前，存戶能　**正解 (A)**
怎麼辦？

(A) 使用臨時銀行。
(B) 等候數天，直到新銀行蓋好。
(C) 在Greydon信託開支票戶。
(D) 打電話給聯邦存款保險公司提領存款。

165

How about the depositors' files and records ?

(A) They were in a safe box in the basement.
(B) They were stored in another place.
(C) The money is safe.
(D) The bank is asking for depositors to support bank anyway.

存戶的檔案和記錄情況如何　**正解 (B)**
？

(A) 存放在地下室的保險箱。
(B) 存放在另一個地方。
(C) 錢是安全的。
(D) 銀行要求存戶無論如何要支持銀行。

166

Why is the depositor's money available?

(A) It is insured.
(B) It was in a separate vault.
(C) Donations will cover most of it.
(D) With depositor's support the bank will not suffer.

何以存戶可動用存款？　　　　**正解 (A)**

(A) 它投保了。
(B) 它放在別的庫房。
(C) 捐款可以支付大部份的錢。
(D) 有存戶的支持，銀行不會損失。

Word Bank

- unusual　*a.* 不正常的，稀少的
- permanent　*a.* 永久的，長久的，固定的
- safe box　保險箱
- available　*a.* 可用的，可獲得的
- vault　*n.* 金庫，保險庫
- suffer　*v.* 受損失，受損害

- rebuild　*v.* 重建
- withdraw　*v.* 提款，撤回
- basement　*n.* 地下室
- separate　*a.* 分開的
- donation　*n.* 捐贈，捐款

Questions 167-170 refer to the following letter.

Dear Sir or Madam,

First of all, we at Via San Remo would like to extend our deepest gratitude for your continued patronage throughout the years. We find that, in these difficult economic times, the cost of maintaining the restaurant at the level at which we have served the community far exceeds projected revenue in the future. Thus, with deep regret, we are closing our doors after 25 years of business in the area.

We will be open for business, with regular business hours, until June 30th. Again, we'd like to thank you and we hope to see you once again. You have been a valued customer and we will surely miss you, your family and guests.

Sincerely,
the Management

問題 **167-170** 請參考以下的信件。

親愛的先生／女士：

首先，我們在Via San Remo，對您多年來持續的惠顧，致上我們最大的謝意。我們發現在這景氣低迷的時候，餐廳若要維持我們向來服務大眾的水準，費用將遠超過未來預期的收入。因此深感遺憾地，我們即將關閉在此地經營了25年的生意。

我們將營業到6月30日，營業時間照常。我們要再次感謝您，並期待有緣再相會。您一直是我們重視的顧客，我們必定會想念您和您的家人、友人。

管理部門敬上

167

What is the purpose of this letter?

(A) To announce a grand opening.
(B) To introduce new management staff.
(C) To inform of a closing.
(D) To notify customers of new business hours.

這封信的目的為何？　　　正解 **(C)**

(A) 宣佈盛大的開幕。
(B) 介紹新的管理員工。
(C) 歇業通知。
(D) 通知顧客新的營業時間。

168

What is this business' current situation?

(A) It is located in a bad area.
(B) It is re-opening elsewhere.
(C) It is undergoing financial difficulties.
(D) Its management has quit.

這家公司目前情況如何？　　正解 **(C)**

(A) 位於很差的地區。
(B) 在其它地方重新開幕。
(C) 正遭逢經濟困境。
(D) 管理階層辭職。

169

What kind of person will receive this letter?

(A) A regular customer.
(B) A picky customer.
(C) Someone who comes in for the first time.
(D) Someone who gets acquainted with the manager.

誰會收到這封信？　　　　正解 **(A)**

(A) 一位常客。
(B) 一位挑剔的顧客。
(C) 第一次來的人。
(D) 和經理相識的人。

170

Who is this letter from?

(A) The owner.
(B) The host and hostess.
(C) The managing staff.
(D) The head chef.

誰發出這封信？　　　　　　　正解 **(C)**

(A) 老闆。
(B) 男主人和女主人。
(C) 管理人員。
(D) 主廚。

Word Bank

- extend　　　　*v.* 給，伸展，擴大
- continued　　　*a.* 繼續的，持續的
- throughout　*prep.* 在…期間
- serve　　　　*v.* 服務
- exceed　　　　*v.* 超過，超出
- revenue　　　　*n.* 收入，歲收
- regular　　　　*a.* 正常的，規劃的，定期的
- surely　　　　*adv.* 確實地
- Sincerely, Sincerely yours, Yours sincerely　謹啟，謹上（信尾客套語）
- owner　　　　*n.* 所有人，擁有者
- hostess　　　　*n.* 女主人，空中小姐
- head chef　　　　主廚
- gratitude　　*n.* 感謝，感激
- patronage　　*n.* 惠顧
- maintain　　*v.* 維持，支持
- community　*n.* 大眾，公眾，社區
- projected　　*a.* 設想的，計劃的
- regret　　　*n.* 遺憾，懊悔
- valued　　　*a.* 重視的，尊重的
- guest　　　　*n.* 客人，賓客
- host　　　　*n.* 主人，主辦人，節目主持人

220

Questions 171-174 refer to the following recipe.

Tahini (Sesame Paste) Salad Dressing

- 2 cloves fresh garlic, crushed
- Half-cup sesame paste
- Quarter-cup soy sauce
- Quarter-cup lemon juice
- Half cup virgin olive oil
- Quarter-cup water
- 1 teaspoon ground cayenne pepper
- 1 teaspoon black pepper

In a saucepan, sauté the fresh, crushed garlic in the olive oil. Do this as slowly as possible and at the lowest flame so that the garlic flavor comes out into the oil as much as possible and because virgin olive oil has a very delicate flavor that can be ruined by too much heat.

Combine the sesame paste and water in a mixing bowl and mix with a wire whisk until creamy smooth with no lumps. Doing this before adding other ingredients makes the sesame paste easier to handle. Add the soy sauce and lemon juice and cayenne and black pepper. When the garlic has sautéed for as long as possible, but before turning brown, add the garlic and olive oil, and whisk until evenly mixed. Drizzle on your favorite salads, or even on fresh, steaming bread.

問題 **171-174** 請參考以下的食譜。

Tahini（芝麻醬）沙拉調味醬

- 兩瓣新鮮大蒜，搗碎
- 半杯芝麻醬
- 1/4杯醬油
- 1/4杯檸檬汁
- 半杯新鮮橄欖油
- 1/4杯水
- 1茶匙磨碎的辣椒粉
- 1茶匙黑胡椒

　　將橄欖油倒入平底鍋，把搗碎的新鮮大蒜拌炒一下。盡可能用最小火慢炒，讓大蒜的味道儘量溶入油裡，因為溫度過高，會破壞新鮮油美好的風味。

　　將芝麻醬和水倒入碗中，用攪拌器攪拌，一直攪到沒有結塊、呈現柔滑乳狀為止。在加入其他材料之前，要先做好芝麻醬，讓它容易料理。再加入醬油、檸檬汁、辣椒粉和黑胡椒。大蒜要炒得愈久愈好，但轉成褐色之前，要加入大蒜和橄欖油，並充分攪拌。可以淋在你喜歡的沙拉，或新鮮剛出爐的麵包上。

中　文　翻　譯　和　解　答

171

Why should the sauté heat be low?

(A) So that you can follow the other directions at the same time.
(B) So you don't burn the pan.
(C) To keep the flavor of the garlic and olive oil best.
(D) To conserve resources.

為何煎炒時要用低溫？　　正解 **(C)**

(A) 以便同時遵照其他指示說明。
(B) 不至於把平底鍋燒焦。
(C) 保持大蒜和橄欖油的最佳風味。
(D) 保存資源。

172

How long should you mix the sesame paste?

(A) Until it is bubbly.
(B) For 5 to 7 minutes.
(C) As long as is needed.
(D) Until it has no lumps.

芝麻醬應攪拌多久？　　正解 **(D)**

(A) 直到起泡。
(B) 5到7分鐘。
(C) 需要多久就多久。
(D) 直到沒有結塊。

173

Why should you mix the sesame paste and water before other ingredients?

(A) The other ingredients will ruin the flavor.
(B) The sesame paste will become easier to work with.
(C) The sesame paste will become richer.
(D) The other ingredients get in the way.

為何放其他材料之前，要先　正解 **(B)**
拌好芝麻醬和水？

(A) 其他材料會破壞它的風味。
(B) 芝麻醬會比較容易料理。
(C) 芝麻醬的營養會更豐富。
(D) 其他材料會有所妨礙。

174

Fllowing the recipe's instructions, what can one make ?

(A) sesame paste
(B) salad dressing
(C) pepper sauce
(D) sautéed garlic

照著這食譜的指示，可以做 **正解 (B)** 出什麼？

(A) 芝麻醬
(B) 莎拉調味醬
(C) 胡椒醬
(D) 油煎大蒜

Word Bank

• recipe	n. 食譜	• sesame	n. 芝麻
• paste	n. 糊狀，膏狀物	• salad dressing	沙拉調味醬
• clove	n. 小球莖	• garlic	n. 大蒜
• crush	v. 弄碎，壓扁	• quarter	n. 1/4(四分之一)
• virgin	a. 新鮮的	• olive oil	橄欖油
• ground	a. 絞碎的，碾碎的	• cayenne (pepper)	n. (紅)辣椒(粉)
• saucepan	n. 深平底鍋	• sauté	v. (用少油)快炒，快煎
• flame	n. 火焰	• delicate	a. 美味的，精巧易碎的
• ruin	v. 破壞	• whisk	n. 攪拌器，打蛋器
• creamy	a. 乳狀的，光滑細膩的	• lump	n. 結塊，腫塊
• ingredient	n. 食材，成分	• soy sauce	醬油
• evenly	adv. 平均地，相等地	• drizzle	v. 下毛毛雨，滴淋
• conserve	v. 保存，保留	• resource	n. 資源，來源
• bubbly	a. 有泡沫的	• get in the way	妨礙，阻擋
• instruction	n. 指示		

原　文　/　中　文　翻　譯

Questions 175-176 refer to the following memo.

MEMO

DATE:　October 11, 2008
TO:　　All Employees
FROM: Carol Katster, Operations Manager

This is to notify you that as of Monday, Octorber 18, our telephone system will be fully automated. We will no longer have operators nor a main switchboard. The Human Resources Department will field misdirected calls but will not take messages of any sort. You are responsible for the automated greetings of your personal line and the retrieval of any messages. Please refer to the message center manual that was distributed last week. For further information, please contact your department manager.

問題 **175-176** 請參考以下的公文。

MEMO

日期: 2008年10月11日
收件人：全體員工
寄件人：營運部經理Carol Katster

我在此通知大家，我們的電話系統將於10月18日（週一）起全面自動化，不再有接線生或總機人員。人力資源部將處理打錯的電話，但不接受任何留言。你們要自己負責處理個人專線的問候語與聽取留言。請參考上週分發的留言中心手冊。若需要進一步資料，請與各部門經理聯繫。

175

What is scheduled to take place?

(A) The notification of all employees.
(B) The firing of all telephone personnel.
(C) The automation of their phone system.
(D) The distribution of new telephone lines.

什麼事情預定要進行？ **正解 (C)**

(A) 通知所有員工。
(B) 開除所有電話業務人員。
(C) 電話系統自動化。
(D) 配置新電話線。

176

What will the Human Resources Department do?

(A) Explain the new system.
(B) Leave message for interviewees.
(C) Pick up certain phone calls.
(D) Leave messages for employees.

人力資源部門將做什麼事？ **正解 (C)**

(A) 解說新系統。
(B) 留話給接受面試者。
(C) 接聽特定電話。
(D) 留話給員工。

Word Bank

· operations manager	營運部經理	· notify	*v.*	通知，公告
· automate	*v.* 使自動化	· operator	*n.*	總機，接線生
· switchboard	*n.* 電話總機	· human resources department 人力資源部		
· field	*v.* (巧妙地)回答	· misdirect	*v.*	誤引，錯用，誤導
· responsible	*a.* 負責的，有責任的	· greetings	*n.*	問候，招呼
· retrieval	*n.* 收回，重獲，取回	· refer to		參考
· manual	*n.* 手冊	· distribute	*v.*	分發，分送
· schedule	*v.* 排定時間表	· take place		發生，舉行
· notification	*n.* 通知，公告	· firing	*n.*	開除，解雇，革職
· personnel	*n.* (全體)人員，人事	· automation	*n.*	自動化
· incoming	*a.* 將來臨的	· pick up		收聽，接聽

原　文　／　中　文　翻　譯

Questions 177-180 refer to the following magazine column.

Q:

I have a pit bull puppy that is 2 months old, and is beginning to get too rowdy and hard-to-handle. I want to train him, but I don't want to hit him, because I am afraid that hitting him might make him mean when he gets older. What should I do?

A:　It is true that hitting an animal can sometimes cause it to become ill-tempered. And besides, you love your puppy, right? So why should you hit it? The answer is in alternative methods to correct bad behavior. Being persistent, and using a stern, strong voice is often all that is needed for your puppy to understand just what you mean. Every time your puppy does something you don't like, respond with a stern "NO!" and gently stop your puppy from jumping up on you or biting. You may be surprised at how puppies will learn to read your feelings just by the sound of your voice if you repeat it the exact same way every time. Remember, the key is repetition and persistence!

問題 **177-180** 請參考以下的雜誌專欄。

問:

我有隻兩個月大的小鬥牛犬，它開始變得粗野，很不聽話。我想要訓練它，但不想打它，因為我怕打了它，它長大後會變得很凶猛。我該怎麼做？

答:　毆打動物，的確有時候會造成它們後來變得性情暴躁。何況你也很喜歡你的小狗，不是嗎？所以何必打它呢？答案就是要採用其他的方法，去矯正不好的行為。要持續用嚴厲堅定的口氣，讓小狗了解你的意思。每次小狗做出你不喜歡的事情，就要嚴厲地說：「不！」；同時很溫和地阻止小狗跳到你身上或咬你。如果你一再重複使用同樣的方法，你將會感到很驚訝，小狗竟然會透過你的聲音，學著去了解你的感覺。記住，秘訣就是重複與堅持！

177

Why does this person need advice about his or her puppy?

(A) The puppy is unhappy.
(B) The person doesn't like his or her puppy.
(C) The puppy is mean.
(D) The puppy is rowdy.

為何這個人需要有關小狗的 **正解 (D)** 建議？

(A) 小狗不開心。
(B) 這個人不喜歡他的狗。
(C) 小狗很兇惡。
(D) 小狗很粗野。

178

Why doesn't this person want to hit his or her puppy?

(A) It hurts the hand.
(B) When the puppy grows up it might become mean.
(C) When the puppy grows up it might hit others.
(D) When the puppy is mean, it bites.

為何這個人不想打小狗？ **正解 (B)**

(A) 手會痛。
(B) 小狗長大後可能會變得很兇惡。
(C) 小狗長大後可能會攻擊他人。
(D) 小狗凶惡時會咬人。

179

What is the column's advice?

(A) Repeatedly use a stern voice.
(B) Just hit the puppy, it will be OK.
(C) Hit persistently.
(D) Get rid of the puppy.

這篇專欄有何建議？ **正解 (A)**

(A) 重複使用嚴厲的聲音。
(B) 只要打小狗，就沒問題了。
(C) 持續地打。
(D) 把小狗丟掉。

中　文　翻　譯　和　解　答

180

According to the columm, what may hitting an animal cause it?

根據此專欄，毆打動物可能導致什麼？ 正解 **(C)**

(A) To become limped.
(B) To become nervous.
(C) To become irritable.
(D) To become friendly.

(A) 變成跛腳。
(B) 變得緊張。
(C) 變得暴躁。
(D) 變得友善。

Word Bank

• magazine column	雜誌專欄	• pit bull puppy	小鬥牛㹴犬
• rowdy	*a.* 粗暴的，吵鬧的	• hard-to-handle	*a.* 難以處理、管理的
• mean	*a.* 兇惡的，卑鄙的	• ill-tempered	脾氣暴躁的
• alternative	*a.* 其他選擇的	• method	*n.* 方法
• behavior	*n.* 行為	• persistent	*a.* 持續的，堅持的
• stern	*a.* 嚴厲的，苛刻的	• puppy	*n.* 小狗
• bite	*v.* 咬	• repetition	*n.* 重覆
• persistence	*n.* 持之以恆，堅持	• repeatedly	*adv.* 重複地
• persistently	*adv.* 持續地	• get rid of ~	除去，戒除

Questions 181-185 refer to the following advertisement and announcement.

USED BOOK SALE

Jeffrey's Used Book Warehouse is having its biggest sale ever. The books have piled up so high that there is almost no room to move around here anymore; so all books are on sale! Especially non-fiction! While all fiction is at least 40 percent off, non-fiction is at least 65 percent off ! Some non-fiction as much as 80 percent off ! Our huge store has so many books that you are sure to find something you like! Buy five books and get one free (priced lower than 12 dollars) ! Sale ends at the end of next week.

Due to the confusion over our former library borrowing policy, Roosevelt County Public Library will be revising its system. While reference books were available for checkout on Fridays before (to be returned the following Monday), starting next week all reference will be for use in the library only. All fiction will be available for a one-month checkout period as opposed to the 5 week checkout before. Nonfiction checkout will remain unchanged. Thank you and keep reading!

問題 **181-185** 請參考以下的廣告和公告。

二手書拍賣

Jeffrey的二手書倉庫，現在正舉辦特優惠大拍賣。
本店的書堆積如山，店內已是寸步難移，
因此所有的書全部便宜賣！尤其是非小
說類！所有小說類都打六折以上，
非小說類至少打三五折！有些非小
說類甚至二折賣出。本店地廣書
多，保證你一定能找到喜歡的書。
買五本再送一本（低於12元的一本
書）！特賣活動至下週末為止。

由於我們原先的圖書借閱制度混淆不清，羅斯福郡公共圖

書館將重新修訂辦法。雖然以前參考書籍可以在週五外借

（隔週一歸還），但從下週起，所有參考書只能在館內使用

。所有小說類書籍，外借時間為一個月，而非之前的五週。

非小說類書籍的借閱時間將維持不變。謝謝各位並請繼續閱

讀！

181

Why is Jeffrey's bookstore having a sale?

(A) The manager said so.
(B) They have too many books.
(C) They want to get more customers.
(D) They like to have sales.

為何Jeffrey的書店要打折？ 正解 **(B)**

(A) 經理說的。
(B) 他們有太多書。
(C) 他們要吸引更多顧客。
(D) 他們喜歡拍賣。

182

Why has the library's system changed?

(A) The librarians were bored with the old system.
(B) The old system confused people.
(C) The old system angered people.
(D) The librarians wanted change.

圖書館的制度為何改變？ 正解 **(B)**

(A) 圖書館員對舊制感到厭煩。
(B) 舊制讓人混淆不清。
(C) 舊制令人生氣。
(D) 圖書館員想要改變。

· librarian   *n.* 圖書館員   · be bored with ~   對～感到厭煩

183

If you bought five books, which book could you get for free?

(A) A fiction book
(B) A book priced lower than twelve dollars
(C) A non-fiction book
(D) Any one of them

如果你買五本書，哪本書可 正解 **(B)**
以免費？

(A) 小說類
(B) 低於12元的一本書
(C) 非小說類的書
(D) 其中任何一本書

中 文 翻 譯 和 解 答

184

How long could reference books be checked out?

(A) for one day
(B) for one week
(C) for two weeks
(D) for the weekend

從前參考書可以借出多久？ 　**正解** (D)

(A) 一天
(B) 一週
(C) 兩週
(D) 一個週末

185

How many weeks will all fiction be available for checkout?

(A) Four week
(B) Five weeks
(C) Two weeks
(D) Three weeks

小說類的出借期間是幾週？ 　**正解** (A)

(A) 四週
(B) 五週
(C) 兩週
(D) 三週

Word Bank

· warehouse	*n.* 倉庫		· pile	*v.* 成堆，堆放
· fiction	*n.* 小說類		· purchase	*v.* 購買，採購
· announcement	*n.* 公告，宣佈		· due to ~	由於～
· confusion	*n.* 混淆，混亂		· policy	*n.* 政策，制度
· revise	*v.* 改變，修訂		· reference	*n.* 參考
· checkout	*n.* 外借，結帳，退房		· as opposed to ~	而不是～
· remain	*v.* 保持，留下			

Questions 186-190 refer to the following e-mails.

To:	Book Club Online [order-info@globalview.com]
From:	borisfrette@iphone.com
Subject:	Replacement & Reimbursement
Date:	Sept. 25, 2008

To whom it may concern,

On September 18th I ordered a copy of Deception Point by Dan Brown and a copy of Four Past Midnight by Stephen King under my order number LW2503.

On opening the package received this afternoon, I found that it contained a copy of Different Seasons and a copy of The Green Mile by the same author, Stephen King. I regret that I can't keep these books as I have bought them already. Therefore I am returning these books by express post for immediate replacement, as I am really looking forward to reading the books I ordered.

By the way, I also hope that you would reimburse $3, the postage, for the returned books. Please check your order records, and send the replacement ASAP.

Faithfully yours,

Boris Frette

To:	borisfrette@iphone.com
From:	Book Club Online [order-info@globalview.com]
Subject:	Re: Replacement & Reimbursement
Date:	Sept. 26, 2008

Dear Mr. Frette,

　　We are very sorry to learn from your e-mail yesterday that a mistake in dealing with your order was made. The mistake is entirely our own. I sincerely apologize for our neglect and the inconvenience caused to you. This occurred during this unusually busy season and also the fact that our staff were exhausted.

　　Two copies of the correct title have been sent to you today. Surely your account will be credited with the invoiced value of the books and the cost of the return postage.

　　Our credit note is enclosed and we apologize again for our mistake.

Sincerely yours,

Andrew Clave

Manager, Service Center
Book Club Online

----- Original Message -----
From: borisfrette@iphone.com
To: Book Club Online [order-info@globalview.com]
Sent: Sept. 25, 2008 2:32 PM
Subject: Replacement & Reimbursement

問題 **186-190** 請參考以下的電子郵件。

收件人：	線上圖書俱樂部 [order-info@globalview.com]
寄件人：	borisfrette@iphone.com
主　旨：	換貨及求償
日　期：	2008年9月25日

敬啟者：

　　9月18日，我訂購一本Dan Brown著的 Deception Point 和一本 Stephen King 寫的 Four Past Midnight，訂單號碼為 LW2503。

　　今天下午我一打開收到的包裹，發現裡面裝的是一本 Different Seasons 和一本 The Green Mile，同樣都是 Stephen King 的著作。很抱歉我不能收下，因為我早已買了這兩本書。所以為了要立即換貨，我要以快遞退回，因為我很期待閱讀我所訂的兩本書。

　　順便提起：我希望你們能補償 3 美元的退書快遞費用。請查證你們的訂貨記錄，同時儘快換書寄來。

衷心問候

Brois Frette

試　題　原　文

收件人 ：	borisfrette@iphone.com
寄件人 ：	線上圖書俱樂部 [order-info@globalview.com]
主　旨 ：	回覆：換貨及求償
日　期 ：	2008年9月26日

親愛的Frette先生：

　　從昨天您的電子郵件中，得知您的訂單發生錯誤，我們甚感抱歉。這完全是我們的錯誤。我為我們的疏忽，和造成您的不便，誠心向您致歉。現在正當旺季，我們異常忙碌，員工也疲憊不堪，因而發生這個錯誤。

　　今天我們已將兩本正確的訂書寄給您。當然您退貨的運費，將從您的帳面上扣除。

　　隨函附上換貨單，同時再度為我們的錯誤向您致歉。

誠摯問候

線上圖書俱樂部
服務中心 經理
Andrew Clave

----- Original Message -----
From: borisfrette@iphone.com
To: Book Club Online [order-info@globalview.com]
Sent: Sept. 25, 2008 2:32 PM
Subject: Replacement & Reimbursement

186

What did Boris ask for?

(A) Paying back partially
(B) Full repayment
(C) Placing an order
(D) Exchanging book

Boris要求什麼？　　　　正解 (D)

(A) 部份退錢
(B) 全額退款
(C) 下訂單
(D) 調換書

・partially　*adv.* 部份地

・exchange　*v.* 調換（商品）

187

Who is the writer of Four Past Midnight?

(A) Boris Frette
(B) Andrew Clave
(C) Stephen King
(D) Dan Brown

Four Past Midnight的作者是何人？　　正解 (C)

(A) Boris Frette
(B) Andrew Clave
(C) Stephen King
(D) Dan Brown

188

Which of the books did Mr. Frette NOT order?

(A) Deception Point
(B) The Green Mile
(C) Four Past Midnight
(D) Book Club Online

Frette先生沒訂哪一本書？　　正解 (B)

(A) Deception Point
(B) The Green Mile
(C) Four Past Midnight
(D) 線上圖書俱樂部

・order　*v.* 訂貨

・online　*a.* 上網的，網路的

中 文 翻 譯 和 解 答

189

Why was the error made?

(A) The staff were dog-tired.
(B) The credit note was not enclosed.
(C) The package was broken.
(D) The order was cancelled.

何以出差錯？

(A) 員工累壞了。
(B) 未附換貨單。
(C) 包裹破了。
(D) 訂單取消。

正解 (A)

- error　*n.* 錯誤

- dog-tired　*a.* 極疲累的

190

When are the correct books delivered?

(A) Sept. 25
(B) Sept. 26
(C) Sept. 18
(D) afternoon, Sep. 18

正確的訂書何時寄送？

(A) 9月25日
(B) 9月26日
(C) 9月18日
(D) 9月18日下午

正解 (B)

- deliver　*v.* 投遞，寄送

Word Bank

- package　*n.* 包裹
- replacement　*n.* 替換，更換
- mistake　*n.* 錯誤
- inconvenience　*n.* 不便
- credit　*v.* 把…入帳

- contain　*v.* 包含，包括
- reimburse　*v.* 償還
- neglect　*n.* 忽略，疏忽
- exhaust　*v.* 耗盡
- invoice　*v.* 向…寄送發票(發貨清單)

Questions 191-195 refer to the following e-mails.

To:	service@daffodilrest.com
From:	doberna@hotonline.net
Subject:	Complaints
Date:	September 7, 2008

To the Manager:

My family and I have been regular customers at your establishment for the last seven years. I have always enjoyed not only the food but also the friendly atmosphere and outstanding service.

On Friday, September 5, I was quite shocked to find that you had completely changed your menu and hired a completely new staff without informing your customers. I was told that your restaurant had not been sold but that management had decided to give the restaurant a "facelift" in order to compete with the trendy new restaurant in town.

First of all, it is hard to believe that you gave no notice whatsoever to your customers about all this. Secondly, and more importantly, I see no reason for such drastic changes. You have a sizable base of loyal, satisfied customers who you will surely lose. The new restaurant in town is good but it is a chain restaurant that lacks the home cooking and the home-like atmosphere that were unique to the Daffodil.

We hope you will reconsider the changes you've made at the Daffodil.

Sincerely,

Donald Berna

To:	doberna@hotonline.net
From:	service@daffodilrest.com
Subject:	Re: Complaints
Date:	September 9, 2008

Dear Mr. Berna,

First and foremost, we deeply appreciate this opportunity to show our heartfelt thanks to you for your concern and continued patronage.

The number of restaurants in this area has greatly increased throughout the past few years. Where there used to be family restaurants serving standard American food for example, is now a restaurant row with Mexican, Indian, Japanese, Filipino and Cuban restaurants, just to name a few. The Daffodil has to compete in a commercial environment so we have transformed it into an American style Italian dinnerhouse.

We regret any inconvenience caused by the change of the Daffodil. You are still a valued customer and we are looking forward to your business.

Sincerely yours,

Darren Carmil

Senior Manager, **The Daffodil**

----- Original Message -----
From: doberna@hotonline.net
To: service@daffodilrest.com
Sent: Sept. 7, 2008 3:02 PM
Subject: Complaints

問題 **191-195** 請參考以下的電子郵件。

收件人：	service@daffodilrest.com
寄件人：	doberna@hotonline.net
主　旨：	抱怨
日　期：	2008年9月7日

致經理：

　　我和我的家人在過去七年來，一直是你們餐廳的常客。我一直都很喜歡你們的料理、親切的氣氛還有非常優質的服務。

　　在週五，即九月五日，我相當驚訝，發現你們已經全面更換菜單，並且僱用全新的人員，但卻沒有告知顧客。有人告訴我餐廳並沒有轉賣，但管理階層為了和城裡新開的時尚餐廳競爭，而決定改裝餐廳。

　　首先，我很難相信，你們竟然沒有將這一切告知顧客們。其次，也是更重要的，我看不出有任何理由要做這麼大幅的改變。你們一定會失去一群原先對你們感到滿意且忠實的廣大顧客。城裡新的餐廳固然不錯，但它是家連鎖餐廳，缺少了家常料理，以及像家的氣氛，而那正是Daffodil餐廳先前的獨特之處。我們希望你重新考慮對Daffodil所做的改變。

祝好

Donald Berna

試　題　原　文

收件人：	doberna@hotonline.net
寄件人：	service@daffodilrest.com
主　旨：	回覆：抱怨
日　期：	2008年9月9日

親愛的Berna先生：

　　首先，我們深深感謝有這個機會，對您的關懷和持續的惠顧，表示我們衷心的謝意。

　　過去幾年來，在這個地區的餐廳大幅增加。以前這裡都是提供標準美式餐點的家庭式餐廳，現在則是一整排墨西哥、印度、日本、菲律賓和古巴等各種餐廳，這只是隨便舉幾個例子。Daffodil餐廳在商業環境中不得不競爭，所以我們把它改造成一家美式義大利餐廳。

　　我們對Daffodil餐廳的改變所造成的任何不便，深感遺憾。您仍然是我們重視的顧客，同時我們將期待您的惠顧。

誠摯問候
Darren Carmil
Daffodil餐廳資深經理

----- Original Message -----
From: doberna@hotonline.net
To: service@daffodilrest.com
Sent: Sept. 7, 2008 3:02 PM
Subject: Complaints

191

What is the general tone of the first e-mail?

(A) Congratulatory
(B) Malicious
(C) Disappointed
(D) Sympathetic

第一封電子郵件整體的語氣為何 正解 **(C)**
？

(A) 祝賀的
(B) 惡意的
(C) 失望的
(D) 同情的

192

What is NOT the Daffodil known for?

(A) Nice meals.
(B) A chain restaurant.
(C) The home cooking.
(D) The home-like atmosphere.

Daffodil餐廳不是以什麼聞名？ 正解 **(B)**

(A) 好吃的餐飲
(B) 連鎖餐廳
(C) 家常料理
(D) 像家的氣氛

193

What troubles Mr. Berna most?

(A) The Daffodil did not notify its customers.
(B) The Daffodil decided to change locations.
(C) The Daffodil decided to close.
(D) The Daffodil totally changed.

什麼事最困擾Berna先生？ 正解 **(D)**

(A) Daffodil並未告知顧客。
(B) Daffodil決定變更地點。
(C) Daffodil決定歇業。
(D) Daffodil完全改變。

中　文　翻　譯　和　解　答

194

When has the increase in international restaurants occurred?

異國餐廳何時開始增加？　　正解 **(B)**

(A) In the past 7 years
(B) In the past few years
(C) On the weekends
(D) In September

(A) 過去七年內
(B) 過去幾年內
(C) 在週末
(D) 在九月

· occur　*v.* 發生

195

What has this area like in the past?

這地區以前情況如何？　　正解 **(D)**

(A) Only Americans lived here.
(B) There used to be a lot of traffic.
(C) There were many fast food restaurants.
(D) There were many family restaurants.

(A) 只有美國人住在此地。
(B) 以前交通繁忙。
(C) 有很多速食店。
(D) 有很多家庭式餐廳。

· traffic　*n.* 交通，行人車輛

Word Bank

· outstanding	*a.* 傑出的，顯著的	· establishment	*n.* 機構，單位，企業
· compete	*v.* 競爭	· facelift	*n.* 翻新，改裝
· trendy	*a.* 時髦的	· whatsoever	*a.* 無論如何
· sizable	*a.* 相當大的	· loyal	*a.* 忠誠的
· lack	*v.* 缺乏	· unique	*a.* 獨特的
· heartfelt	*a.* 衷心的	· concern	*n.* 關懷
· patronage	*n.* 惠顧	· compete	*v.* 競爭
· commercial	*a.* 商業的	· environment	*n.* 環境
· transform	*v.* 改造	· inconvenience	*n.* 不便

Questions 196-200 refer to the following letters.

Dear Mr. Waltin,

This is to formally invite you to the reception of our company's 28th anniversary celebration which I have already mentioned to you by phone last week. The reception will be held in the International Convention Hall of the New Oriental Hotel. The formal invitation will be sent to you by express this afternoon.

The purpose of this reception is just to invite some of the important people who have supported us over the years so that we can show a small token of our gratitude.

We do hope that you will be able to spare the time to share this historical moment with us.

Sincerely yours,

Lois Vinster

Lois Vinster
Vice president,
Stastech Ltd Company

Dear Ms. Vinster,

No doubt there will be celebration taking place next month at your corporate headquarters, I would like to join those wishing you heartiest congratulations on your 28 years serving the automotive needs of Singaporean consumers.

As a major supplier to your firm for the past 12 years, we appreciate having had the opportunity to help position you as one of the preeminent manufacturers of automotive parts in the country. It has been a beneficial journey for both our firms, and we are glad to have been part of the excitement.

A toast to you on your 28th anniversary! Here's hoping the next 28 years will be even more successful for all of us.

Best regards,

Derek Waltin

Derek Waltin
Senior Vice President,
Cartech Company

問題 **196-200** 請參考以下的信件。

親愛的Waltin先生：

　　在此正式邀請您參加我們公司的28週年慶祝會，在上星期我曾以電話跟您提過這件事。宴會將在 New Oriental 飯店的國際會議廳舉行。正式的邀請函將於今天下午以快遞送去給您。

　　此次宴會的目的就是想邀請多年來一直支持我們的重要人士，藉此略表我們的謝意。

　　深切盼望您能撥冗和我們分享這歷史性的時刻。

誠摯問候

　　　　　　　　　　　　　　　　Stastech 股份有限公司
　　　　　　　　　　　　　　　　副總經理

　　　　　　　　　　　　　　　　Lois Vinster

　　　　　　　　　　　　　　　　Lois Vinster

　　　　　　　　　　　　　　　　　　　　　　敬上

試　　題　　原　　文

親愛的Vinster女士：

　　下個月貴公司總部將舉行慶祝會，毫無疑問地，我也和大家一樣，向你們致上最誠摯的祝賀，恭喜你們為新加坡的消費者提供汽車需求的服務，已達28年。

　　過去12年來，作為貴公司的主要供應商，我們很感謝有這機會，協助你們成為國內傑出的汽車零件製造商。這對我們雙方的公司都是有所獲益的過程，而我們很高興能共沾喜氣。

　　恭賀你們28週年慶！希望再下一個28年我們彼此更加成功。

誠摯問候

*Cartech*公司
資深副總經理

Derek Waltin

Derek Waltin

敬上

196

Who is the writer of the second letter? 　　寫第二封信的人是誰？　　正解 **(C)**

(A) A member of a competing firm 　　(A) 對手公司的成員
(B) A manufacturer of auto parts 　　(B) 汽車零件製造商
(C) A supplier of a car parts maker 　　(C) 汽車零件製造廠的供應商
(D) A car manufacturer 　　(D) 汽車廠商

・competing　*a.* 競爭的

197

How long have the two firms been connected? 　　兩家公司合作多久了？　　正解 **(B)**

(A) 28 years 　　(A) 28年
(B) 12 years 　　(B) 12年
(C) 40 years 　　(C) 40年
(D) Not specified 　　(D) 未說明

・connect　*v.* 有關聯，連結　　　・specify　*v.* 具體說明

198

What does Ms. Vinster's firm do? 　　Vinster女士的公司做什麼行業？　正解 **(C)**

(A) Manufactures automobiles 　　(A) 製造汽車
(B) Buys auto parts from manufacturers 　　(B) 向製造商買汽車零件
(C) Manufactures parts for automobiles 　　(C) 製造汽車零件
(D) Supplies parts to an auto parts maker 　　(D) 提供零件給汽車零件製造廠

・auto parts　汽車零件

中 文 翻 譯 和 解 答

199

How many times will Mr. Waltin have been informed of the invitation message?

(A) 1 time
(B) 2 times
(C) 3 times
(D) Not specified

Waltin 先生會被告知邀請的訊息 **正解 (C)** 幾次？

(A) 一次
(B) 兩次
(C) 三次
(D) 未說明

• specify *v.* 具體說明

200

In Vinster's letter, the word " token " in paragraph 2, line 3 is closest in meaning to

(A) symbol
(B) keepsake
(C) lot
(D) coin

在Vinster的信件中，第二段第三 **正解 (A)** 行的單字 "token" 最接近哪個 意思？

(A) 象徵
(B) 小紀念品
(C) 一群（批）
(D) 硬幣

• symbol *n.* 象徵

• keepsake *n.* 小紀念品

Word Bank

• reception	*n.* 招待會，宴會	• anniversary	*n.* 週年紀念日
• mention	*v.* 提及，提到	• invitation	*n.* 請柬，邀請
• a small token of	一點點表示	• gratitude	*n.* 謝意，感激
• spare the time	抽空	• celebration	*n.* 慶祝
• take place	發生	• hearty	*a.* 熱心的，熱忱的
• preeminent	*a.* 卓越的，傑出的	• beneficial	*a.* 有利的，有益的
• journey	*n.* 過程，行程	• excitement	*n.* 興奮，激勵
• successful	*a.* 成功的		

Test Score Conversion Tables

Compare the total number of correct answers (raw score) in each of the listening and reading sections of the test to the appropriate section of the tables below. Add the converted listening and reading scores together to get an estimated total score.

Listening Raw Score	Listening Scaled Score	Reading Raw Score	Reading Scaled Score
96-100	495	96-100	470-495
91-95	450-495	91-95	430-475
86-90	415-475	86-90	405-440
81-85	370-450	81-85	375-420
76-80	340-420	76-80	350-395
71-75	315-390	71-75	325-380
66-70	285-360	66-70	295-350
61-65	255-330	61-65	265-325
56-60	230-305	56-60	235-295
51-55	205-275	51-55	205-270
46-50	175-245	46-50	170-235
41-45	150-220	41-45	140-205
36-40	125-185	36-40	110-175
31-35	100-155	31-35	90-145
26-30	85-120	26-30	70-120
21-25	75-100	21-25	60-90
16-20	55-80	16-20	45-70
11-15	35-65	11-15	35-55
6-10	25-40	6-10	20-40
1-5	10-30	1-5	10-20
0	0	0	5

The practice test in this book is a mock test. Therefore, your score on the practice test may be higher or lower than your score on the actual TOEIC test.

New TOEIC Practice Test : Answer Sheet

Registration Number						
Name						

Part 1

1 Ⓐ Ⓑ Ⓒ Ⓓ
2 Ⓐ Ⓑ Ⓒ Ⓓ
3 Ⓐ Ⓑ Ⓒ Ⓓ
4 Ⓐ Ⓑ Ⓒ Ⓓ
5 Ⓐ Ⓑ Ⓒ Ⓓ
6 Ⓐ Ⓑ Ⓒ Ⓓ
7 Ⓐ Ⓑ Ⓒ Ⓓ
8 Ⓐ Ⓑ Ⓒ Ⓓ
9 Ⓐ Ⓑ Ⓒ Ⓓ
10 Ⓐ Ⓑ Ⓒ Ⓓ

Part 2

11 Ⓐ Ⓑ Ⓒ
12 Ⓐ Ⓑ Ⓒ
13 Ⓐ Ⓑ Ⓒ
14 Ⓐ Ⓑ Ⓒ
15 Ⓐ Ⓑ Ⓒ
16 Ⓐ Ⓑ Ⓒ
17 Ⓐ Ⓑ Ⓒ
18 Ⓐ Ⓑ Ⓒ
19 Ⓐ Ⓑ Ⓒ
20 Ⓐ Ⓑ Ⓒ
21 Ⓐ Ⓑ Ⓒ
22 Ⓐ Ⓑ Ⓒ
23 Ⓐ Ⓑ Ⓒ
24 Ⓐ Ⓑ Ⓒ
25 Ⓐ Ⓑ Ⓒ
26 Ⓐ Ⓑ Ⓒ
27 Ⓐ Ⓑ Ⓒ
28 Ⓐ Ⓑ Ⓒ
29 Ⓐ Ⓑ Ⓒ
30 Ⓐ Ⓑ Ⓒ
31 Ⓐ Ⓑ Ⓒ
32 Ⓐ Ⓑ Ⓒ
33 Ⓐ Ⓑ Ⓒ
34 Ⓐ Ⓑ Ⓒ
35 Ⓐ Ⓑ Ⓒ
36 Ⓐ Ⓑ Ⓒ
37 Ⓐ Ⓑ Ⓒ
38 Ⓐ Ⓑ Ⓒ
39 Ⓐ Ⓑ Ⓒ
40 Ⓐ Ⓑ Ⓒ

Part 3

41 Ⓐ Ⓑ Ⓒ Ⓓ
42 Ⓐ Ⓑ Ⓒ Ⓓ
43 Ⓐ Ⓑ Ⓒ Ⓓ
44 Ⓐ Ⓑ Ⓒ Ⓓ
45 Ⓐ Ⓑ Ⓒ Ⓓ
46 Ⓐ Ⓑ Ⓒ Ⓓ
47 Ⓐ Ⓑ Ⓒ Ⓓ
48 Ⓐ Ⓑ Ⓒ Ⓓ
49 Ⓐ Ⓑ Ⓒ Ⓓ
50 Ⓐ Ⓑ Ⓒ Ⓓ
51 Ⓐ Ⓑ Ⓒ Ⓓ
52 Ⓐ Ⓑ Ⓒ Ⓓ
53 Ⓐ Ⓑ Ⓒ Ⓓ
54 Ⓐ Ⓑ Ⓒ Ⓓ
55 Ⓐ Ⓑ Ⓒ Ⓓ
56 Ⓐ Ⓑ Ⓒ Ⓓ
57 Ⓐ Ⓑ Ⓒ Ⓓ
58 Ⓐ Ⓑ Ⓒ Ⓓ
59 Ⓐ Ⓑ Ⓒ Ⓓ
60 Ⓐ Ⓑ Ⓒ Ⓓ
61 Ⓐ Ⓑ Ⓒ Ⓓ
62 Ⓐ Ⓑ Ⓒ Ⓓ
63 Ⓐ Ⓑ Ⓒ Ⓓ
64 Ⓐ Ⓑ Ⓒ Ⓓ
65 Ⓐ Ⓑ Ⓒ Ⓓ
66 Ⓐ Ⓑ Ⓒ Ⓓ
67 Ⓐ Ⓑ Ⓒ Ⓓ
68 Ⓐ Ⓑ Ⓒ Ⓓ
69 Ⓐ Ⓑ Ⓒ Ⓓ
70 Ⓐ Ⓑ Ⓒ Ⓓ

Part 4

71 Ⓐ Ⓑ Ⓒ Ⓓ
72 Ⓐ Ⓑ Ⓒ Ⓓ
73 Ⓐ Ⓑ Ⓒ Ⓓ
74 Ⓐ Ⓑ Ⓒ Ⓓ
75 Ⓐ Ⓑ Ⓒ Ⓓ
76 Ⓐ Ⓑ Ⓒ Ⓓ
77 Ⓐ Ⓑ Ⓒ Ⓓ
78 Ⓐ Ⓑ Ⓒ Ⓓ
79 Ⓐ Ⓑ Ⓒ Ⓓ
80 Ⓐ Ⓑ Ⓒ Ⓓ
81 Ⓐ Ⓑ Ⓒ Ⓓ
82 Ⓐ Ⓑ Ⓒ Ⓓ
83 Ⓐ Ⓑ Ⓒ Ⓓ
84 Ⓐ Ⓑ Ⓒ Ⓓ
85 Ⓐ Ⓑ Ⓒ Ⓓ
86 Ⓐ Ⓑ Ⓒ Ⓓ
87 Ⓐ Ⓑ Ⓒ Ⓓ
88 Ⓐ Ⓑ Ⓒ Ⓓ
89 Ⓐ Ⓑ Ⓒ Ⓓ
90 Ⓐ Ⓑ Ⓒ Ⓓ
91 Ⓐ Ⓑ Ⓒ Ⓓ
92 Ⓐ Ⓑ Ⓒ Ⓓ
93 Ⓐ Ⓑ Ⓒ Ⓓ
94 Ⓐ Ⓑ Ⓒ Ⓓ
95 Ⓐ Ⓑ Ⓒ Ⓓ
96 Ⓐ Ⓑ Ⓒ Ⓓ
97 Ⓐ Ⓑ Ⓒ Ⓓ
98 Ⓐ Ⓑ Ⓒ Ⓓ
99 Ⓐ Ⓑ Ⓒ Ⓓ
100 Ⓐ Ⓑ Ⓒ Ⓓ

Part 5

101 Ⓐ Ⓑ Ⓒ Ⓓ
102 Ⓐ Ⓑ Ⓒ Ⓓ
103 Ⓐ Ⓑ Ⓒ Ⓓ
104 Ⓐ Ⓑ Ⓒ Ⓓ
105 Ⓐ Ⓑ Ⓒ Ⓓ
106 Ⓐ Ⓑ Ⓒ Ⓓ
107 Ⓐ Ⓑ Ⓒ Ⓓ
108 Ⓐ Ⓑ Ⓒ Ⓓ
109 Ⓐ Ⓑ Ⓒ Ⓓ
110 Ⓐ Ⓑ Ⓒ Ⓓ
111 Ⓐ Ⓑ Ⓒ Ⓓ
112 Ⓐ Ⓑ Ⓒ Ⓓ
113 Ⓐ Ⓑ Ⓒ Ⓓ
114 Ⓐ Ⓑ Ⓒ Ⓓ
115 Ⓐ Ⓑ Ⓒ Ⓓ
116 Ⓐ Ⓑ Ⓒ Ⓓ
117 Ⓐ Ⓑ Ⓒ Ⓓ
118 Ⓐ Ⓑ Ⓒ Ⓓ
119 Ⓐ Ⓑ Ⓒ Ⓓ
120 Ⓐ Ⓑ Ⓒ Ⓓ
121 Ⓐ Ⓑ Ⓒ Ⓓ
122 Ⓐ Ⓑ Ⓒ Ⓓ
123 Ⓐ Ⓑ Ⓒ Ⓓ
124 Ⓐ Ⓑ Ⓒ Ⓓ
125 Ⓐ Ⓑ Ⓒ Ⓓ
126 Ⓐ Ⓑ Ⓒ Ⓓ
127 Ⓐ Ⓑ Ⓒ Ⓓ
128 Ⓐ Ⓑ Ⓒ Ⓓ
129 Ⓐ Ⓑ Ⓒ Ⓓ
130 Ⓐ Ⓑ Ⓒ Ⓓ
131 Ⓐ Ⓑ Ⓒ Ⓓ
132 Ⓐ Ⓑ Ⓒ Ⓓ
133 Ⓐ Ⓑ Ⓒ Ⓓ
134 Ⓐ Ⓑ Ⓒ Ⓓ
135 Ⓐ Ⓑ Ⓒ Ⓓ
136 Ⓐ Ⓑ Ⓒ Ⓓ
137 Ⓐ Ⓑ Ⓒ Ⓓ
138 Ⓐ Ⓑ Ⓒ Ⓓ
139 Ⓐ Ⓑ Ⓒ Ⓓ
140 Ⓐ Ⓑ Ⓒ Ⓓ

Part 6

141 Ⓐ Ⓑ Ⓒ Ⓓ
142 Ⓐ Ⓑ Ⓒ Ⓓ
143 Ⓐ Ⓑ Ⓒ Ⓓ
144 Ⓐ Ⓑ Ⓒ Ⓓ
145 Ⓐ Ⓑ Ⓒ Ⓓ
146 Ⓐ Ⓑ Ⓒ Ⓓ
147 Ⓐ Ⓑ Ⓒ Ⓓ
148 Ⓐ Ⓑ Ⓒ Ⓓ
149 Ⓐ Ⓑ Ⓒ Ⓓ
150 Ⓐ Ⓑ Ⓒ Ⓓ
151 Ⓐ Ⓑ Ⓒ Ⓓ
152 Ⓐ Ⓑ Ⓒ Ⓓ

Part 7

153 Ⓐ Ⓑ Ⓒ Ⓓ
154 Ⓐ Ⓑ Ⓒ Ⓓ
155 Ⓐ Ⓑ Ⓒ Ⓓ
156 Ⓐ Ⓑ Ⓒ Ⓓ
157 Ⓐ Ⓑ Ⓒ Ⓓ
158 Ⓐ Ⓑ Ⓒ Ⓓ
159 Ⓐ Ⓑ Ⓒ Ⓓ
160 Ⓐ Ⓑ Ⓒ Ⓓ
161 Ⓐ Ⓑ Ⓒ Ⓓ
162 Ⓐ Ⓑ Ⓒ Ⓓ
163 Ⓐ Ⓑ Ⓒ Ⓓ
164 Ⓐ Ⓑ Ⓒ Ⓓ
165 Ⓐ Ⓑ Ⓒ Ⓓ
166 Ⓐ Ⓑ Ⓒ Ⓓ
167 Ⓐ Ⓑ Ⓒ Ⓓ
168 Ⓐ Ⓑ Ⓒ Ⓓ
169 Ⓐ Ⓑ Ⓒ Ⓓ
170 Ⓐ Ⓑ Ⓒ Ⓓ
171 Ⓐ Ⓑ Ⓒ Ⓓ
172 Ⓐ Ⓑ Ⓒ Ⓓ
173 Ⓐ Ⓑ Ⓒ Ⓓ
174 Ⓐ Ⓑ Ⓒ Ⓓ
175 Ⓐ Ⓑ Ⓒ Ⓓ
176 Ⓐ Ⓑ Ⓒ Ⓓ
177 Ⓐ Ⓑ Ⓒ Ⓓ
178 Ⓐ Ⓑ Ⓒ Ⓓ
179 Ⓐ Ⓑ Ⓒ Ⓓ
180 Ⓐ Ⓑ Ⓒ Ⓓ
181 Ⓐ Ⓑ Ⓒ Ⓓ
182 Ⓐ Ⓑ Ⓒ Ⓓ
183 Ⓐ Ⓑ Ⓒ Ⓓ
184 Ⓐ Ⓑ Ⓒ Ⓓ
185 Ⓐ Ⓑ Ⓒ Ⓓ
186 Ⓐ Ⓑ Ⓒ Ⓓ
187 Ⓐ Ⓑ Ⓒ Ⓓ
188 Ⓐ Ⓑ Ⓒ Ⓓ
189 Ⓐ Ⓑ Ⓒ Ⓓ
190 Ⓐ Ⓑ Ⓒ Ⓓ
191 Ⓐ Ⓑ Ⓒ Ⓓ
192 Ⓐ Ⓑ Ⓒ Ⓓ
193 Ⓐ Ⓑ Ⓒ Ⓓ
194 Ⓐ Ⓑ Ⓒ Ⓓ
195 Ⓐ Ⓑ Ⓒ Ⓓ
196 Ⓐ Ⓑ Ⓒ Ⓓ
197 Ⓐ Ⓑ Ⓒ Ⓓ
198 Ⓐ Ⓑ Ⓒ Ⓓ
199 Ⓐ Ⓑ Ⓒ Ⓓ
200 Ⓐ Ⓑ Ⓒ Ⓓ

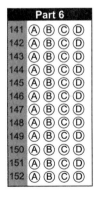

※本空白答案表請讀者自行影印以便於自我測驗

國家圖書館出版品預行編目資料

新多益測驗解析／高志豪著. — 初版. —
臺北市：五南，2016.03
　　面；　公分.
ISBN 978-957-11-8501-9（平裝）

1.多益測驗

805.1895　　　　　　　　105000944

1X8Q

新多益測驗解析

作　　者 — 高志豪

發 行 人 — 楊榮川

總 編 輯 — 王翠華

主　　編 — 黃惠娟

責任編輯 — 蔡佳伶

封面設計 — 陳翰陞

出 版 者 — 五南圖書出版股份有限公司

地　　址：106台北市大安區和平東路二段339號4樓

電　　話：(02)2705-5066　　傳　　真：(02)2706-6100

網　　址：http://www.wunan.com.tw

電子郵件：wunan@wunan.com.tw

劃撥帳號：01068953

戶　　名：五南圖書出版股份有限公司

法律顧問　林勝安律師事務所　林勝安律師

出版日期　2016年 3 月初版一刷

定　　價　新臺幣320元

※版權所有 · 欲利用本書內容，必須徵求本公司同意※